A TIGER IN EDEN

Chris Flynn is books editor at the *Big Issue* and fiction consultant at *Australian Book Review*. The former publisher of *Torpedo* magazine, he writes for the *Age*, the *Australian*, the *Paris Review* and ABC Radio National. He was born in Belfast and lives in Melbourne, and was once a sumo-wrestling referee in a travelling fair.

atigerineden.com

A TIGER IN EDEN

CHRIS FLYNN

TEXT PUBLISHING MELBOURNE AUSTRALIA

textpublishing.com.au

The Text Publishing Company
Swann House
22 William Street
Melbourne Victoria 3000
Australia

Copyright © Chris Flynn, 2012

All rights reserved. Without limiting the rights under copyright above, no part of this publication shall be reproduced, stored in or introduced into a retrieval system, or transmitted in any form or by any means (electronic, mechanical, photocopying, recording or otherwise), without the prior permission of both the copyright owner and the publisher of this book.

First published in 2012 by The Text Publishing Company
Reprinted 2013

Cover and text art and design by W.H. Chong
Typeset by J&M Typesetting
Printed in Australia by Griffin Press, an Accredited ISO AS/NZS 14001:2004 Environmental Management System printer

Primary print ISBN: 9781921922039
Ebook ISBN: 9781921921308

National Library of Australia Cataloguing-in-Publication entry:
Author: Flynn, Chris.
Title: A tiger in eden / Chris Flynn.
ISBN: 9781921922039 (pbk.)
Dewey Number: A823.4

This book is printed on paper certified against the Forest Stewardship Council® Standards. Griffin Press holds FSC chain-of-custody certification SGS-COC-005088. FSC promotes environmentally responsible, socially beneficial and economically viable management of the world's forests.

The weird thing is, right, apart from the fact a good book can take your mind off of things like the past and that, is that I starts speaking different. I could hear myself using words I'd never said before and I was thinking fuck me, I sound all educated or something. Just goes to show you like, I always thought you could never learn nothing from books but I was telling this Scottish lad about it one night at the bar, he was a good Prod so he was, he'd seen Rangers play loads of times, and he says to me sure reading books improves your vocabulary, everyone knows that.

Fuck me, I says, I must of missed the memo.

Aye, he goes, the honeys love it too. You'll not just be getting the superficial women, the intellectual ones'll be chasing you too.

I liked how he was speaking. He was just a normal-looking down-to-earth fella but he had a proper aul brain on him. The ones with glasses and that, I goes, like the sexy librarian type?

Totally, he says, sure they're way better company anyway. I can't be bothered chasing after the bimbos no more, sure do they not do your head in, giggling and laughing and talking shite?

Aye, I suppose so, I goes, I never thought about it like that.

Tell you what, he says, take one of your good books, not some cheesy thriller but a classic maybe or something like that and go lie on the beach next to one of the smart honeys. Don't pay her any attention but just look like you're absorbed in the book.

I always am anyway, I says.

Aye, well there you go, easy enough then, he says. Guaranteed she'll ask you what you're reading and youse'll start up a conversation.

Aye? I goes, what about when she hears me talking? Pretty obvious I'm not signed up to the Mensa like.

Even better, he goes, nothing like a dumb cunt trying to improve himself, no offence like. They'll fucking love it, I'm telling ye.

He was a good lad, I could've hung around with him for ages but he was in and out in a couple of days like most of them. Duncan was his name, I got his address and he said he'd take me to a Rangers game if I was ever in Glasgow. I'd fucking love that, so I would, but the peelers would probably pick me up in five minutes flat if I showed my face at an airport in the UK, it's fucking bollixed, so it is. Sure you won't catch me anywhere near the joint no more.

He was on the money about women liking the books though. And as soon as he says about the bimbos being annoying, sure I went through a period of a couple of months where I couldn't stand the sight of them. I mean, they're good-looking and that but as soon as they open their gobs I just want to walk away. So I found myself attracted to the quieter girls, the ones who weren't looking for all the attention and who were on their own wee trip. The thing about Ko Phi Phi is that there's always people coming and going so just when you think there's no cunt worth talking to, sure the next day a couple more people will turn up.

I fell in with this wee Australian girl. Her hair was dead short and she never walked around in a bikini or nothing. She'd wear them fisherman pants and a wee loose blouse. I seen her playing the guitar down the beach one day and I walked over to get a look at her. She was singing this song and kept stopping to write something down in her black notebook. Sure all the backpackers carry them. Anyway I wandered up and she looks over at me and smiles even though she was still playing the guitar and singing. She'd a fucking lovely voice, you'd never think such a sound would come out of her. The song was beautiful, so it was, something about paradise. She finished up and says hello to me.

Hello yourself, I says, that song was amazing, so it was. Was that Bob Dylan or one of them ones?

She laughs and goes, well thanks for the compliment but no, that was one of mine.

You're kidding me on, I goes. What was it called?

I'm still writing it actually, she says, but I was thinking of calling it 'Lost in Paradise'. Maybe that's a bit too sad though, what do you think?

I sat down on the sand then. There was something about the song and the title of it that made me come over all funny. It hit me hard, so it did. I could almost feel the aul waterworks coming on and truth be told it was all a bit embarrassing.

Are you all right, she says.

Aye, I goes, it's just like I've been here for a while, so I know what you mean.

She nods and looks at me. I was staring down at the cover of the book I'd brought along to try and impress her. It was this mad story about a fella who wakes up one morning to find out he's a big beetle. I felt like a right sad cunt, sitting there feeling sorry for myself.

Are you travelling by yourself, she asks me.

Aye, I says, almost a year now.

Sorry, I didn't mean to upset you, she goes.

You're all right, I says, recovering myself a bit, thinking what the fuck's wrong with you Billy, pull yourself together in front of the wee girl. What about yourself, I says, just you and the guitar is it?

Yeah, she goes, I'm on holidays from uni and I just

had to get away from people.

Aye, I know that feeling, I says. I wish I could play the guitar but I'm not musical at all.

Are you any good with words, she goes, I'm stuck for a rhyme here.

Sure I wouldn't have a clue, I says, I never went to school much.

And yet you're reading Kafka, she goes, pointing it out with the wee guitar pick.

Aye, I like the story, but to be honest some of the words are beyond me. I should of paid more attention in aul Mr Clough's English class, then maybe I wouldn't be in this predicament.

Her face lit up then all sudden like. Hold on, she goes, I'm going to try that, and she sings back a wee bit of the song only the last line was *I wouldn't be in this predicament*. I couldn't believe it. She pumps her fist then and scribbles the words down in her book.

Yes! she goes, that's perfect! You don't mind if I use that line, do you?

No bother, I goes, just talk to my agent about the royalties.

We were like two peas in a pod after that, me and her. I didn't even try it on with her or nothing. I was kind of intimidated by her, I suppose. She was staying in the next resort along the beach, if you could call it that. It was just a bunch of aul huts. Her name was Tanya and she was hanging around for a couple of weeks with no big plans, like a short-term version of myself, that's probably why I liked her.

Loads of the locals in these wee islands in the south are Muslims. It's close to Malaysia I suppose and they're all Muslim down there, sure. I'd never met any before but Tanya says to me there's not that much difference between their bible and ours, not that I believe in all that anyway so I couldn't care less. I tell you one thing, the aul beef massaman the Thai Muslims make is cracker, so it is. If that's what you get when you go to Mecca, sign me up, I says, though when Tanya told me the women have to cover up and that I said I was only joking. That's why she never wandered around in her bikini or topless like some of the backpackers. They were disrespecting the locals, she says. Now I like a bit of aul tit so I argued with her but she goes, imagine if Catholics started marching down your street and sitting in your front garden would you not say something? She was wise by this stage to me being from Belfast, sure she picked it straightaway. Obviously I kept most of it close to my chest but she knew loads about the situation back home, more than me nearly.

Course, I says, I don't want no Fenians, I mean Catholics, parading around in my street, shoving their aul rituals and that in my face.

Well then, she says, how do you think the Muslims feel being brought up that women shouldn't expose themselves and then here all these bimbos are flapping their tits around? I'm not saying I agree with Islam, she goes, I think a woman should have a right to do and wear what she wants, but still, you have to respect what others believe.

I was troubled by what she was saying. I could see the sense in it but it made me think maybe we were doing the wrong thing by the Fenians back home. Sure we're always marching down Catholic streets on the Glorious Twelfth, rubbing their noses in it, saying these are our traditional marching grounds.

I didn't want to think about it too much to be honest but one day soon after, me and Tanya was sitting having a bite of lunch under the trees outside her hut when I said something that got me into a fight. The huts were owned by a family and they would cook for you whenever you wanted. It's the same arrangement all over the place. Anyway, they were dead Muslim and they loved our Tanya. So we were sitting minding our own business and I could see these two girls playing frisbee with this lad on the beach. I could hear from their squealing that they were English. They're playing away and then one of the girls takes her bikini top off. She had quite big tits and I was thinking what's she taking that off for, sure she's running around all over the place trying to catch the frisbee and they were bouncing up and down like nobody's business. Showing off for the man, no doubt. Tanya just shakes her head. I was trying not to look but then they finished up their game and comes wandering up to where we were sitting, right into the wee shelter where you sit down to have something to eat. Sure I couldn't believe it, the English girl didn't even bother putting her bikini top back on. She sees me and she starts smiling and sticking her tits out as if we couldn't already see them. I looked round and there's the Muslim father covering his face and the mother trying to grab the kids, their eyes like dinner plates of course. It was fucking disgraceful, so it was.

Hey, put your top on love, I says, quite angry, you're scaring the weans.

What's that, she goes.

You heard me, I says, cover up, that's not appropriate here. I could see Tanya's eyes narrowing. She was pissed off and all and I was glad I said something. But then this English bitch puts her hands on her hips and starts staring down at her tits like they're the best invention since ashtrays on motorbikes.

It's perfectly natural, she goes, I'm proud of my body and I don't care who sees it. It's not my fault you're a prude.

Love, you don't have a fucking clue about me, I says. Now, you're offending this family so either put your T-shirt on or fuck off and eat somewhere else, all right?

Course the fella steps forward then and tries to act like a hard man, which was pretty difficult for him with his aul annoying sing-song southern accent. You got a problem, mate? he goes. I nearly burst out laughing. Tanya put her hand on my arm, not because she didn't want me to get into a fight but because she'd already seen my NO SURRENDER tattoos and worked out I was a mad cunt. She knew I'd burst his gob.

Youse are the ones with the problems, I goes, what's wrong with you? Show some respect to the locals that are having to put up with ye. Now do the right thing and put your top on darlin', and as for you big man, take a seat and we'll all be friends. You don't want to go down the other road with me.

If they'd an ounce of sense that would of been the end of it but they were young and they didn't like me telling them what to do even if it was the right thing. The girl with her tits out goes, fuck you, Paddy, and I saw red. I threw my plate of rice in her face, it wouldn't of been sore or nothing I just wanted to embarrass her the way she was doing to the family. Tanya put her hand over her mouth trying not to laugh. The lad ran forward to take a swing at me but he was hopeless. I didn't even move, I just let him hit me, sure his punch was piss-weak. My granny used to hit me harder than that when I was a wean.

I stood up then and popped him one in the mouth, not even hard like, I was just playing 'cos I knew he was just a dumb kid. He went down like a ton of bricks. His lip burst on his teeth but sure it looked worse than it was. He rolled around squealing, holding his face like he was appealing to the ref for a penalty. The girl just stood there, fried rice dripping all over her stupid tits. You, I says dead loud to her friend, sure she near jumped out of her skin, put the T-shirt on her, gather your man there and away to fuck the lot of ye.

Right enough she jumped to it.

When are youse leaving, I goes to her as she pulls the top on over her stunned pal.

After the weekend, she says, shaking.

Wrong answer, I goes, try again.

Tomorrow? she stammers.

If you hurry up, there's a ferry going back to Krabi tonight, I says, I advise you to be on it. I don't want to see your faces round here no more.

The one with the rice on her gob still had a wee bit of fight in her and she goes, we're going to tell the police about you.

This is Thailand, love, I says to her, catch yourself on. I could drag the three of youse out to sea, hold your heads down three times and bring them up twice and sure the peelers wouldn't say nothing. Show some respect in the future and you won't get into trouble. Youse are lucky I'm in a good mood otherwise this might of ended much worse for the three of ye today. Now go on.

Off they went with their tails between their legs. I apologised to the family that run the place but the father was slapping me on the back like I was a hero or something, he said I'd make a good Muslim. Aye, I says, just pay us back in beef massaman and I'm sorted. The funny thing is, the whole time I was thinking how fucking weird was that. Tanya, I goes, you're a bad influence on me, sure that's the first time in my life I told a girl off for getting her tits out. That's contrary to my nature.

Tanya laughed and winked at me. Plenty more tits in the sea, she goes.

I tell you what, I fairly missed Tanya after she was gone back to Australia. Sure I learned more from her in those two weeks than I had in years at school back home. It was dead sad when she had to go. I was never pals with someone so young who knew so much about the world. It was an eye-opener for me and I decided to watch out for others like her. I felt like I was from some fucking backwater compared to her.

She gave me her address in Cairns and said I should come out and see her when she next had holidays, that we'd go diving on the Barrier Reef. It sounded like another planet. I told her I'd try and I put it to the back of my mind to have an aul think about.

Thailand was all very well, but I couldn't stay here forever without going mad. I was starting to get a wee taste that there might be other places I wouldn't mind seeing. I'd just have to work out how to do it without getting pulled up by the peelers. I couldn't exactly jump on the aul British Airways wearing a false beard or something, that wasn't going to cut it like.

Me and Tanya hung out the whole day together on her last day. She comes round to my hut dead early, it was still dark outside but it was a hot night. I put a towel round me and opened the door wondering who the fuck it was. She squeezed in and says, are you awake?

Aye, sure I had to get up to answer the door, I says, what's wrong?

Nothing, she goes, I just want to go for a walk on the beach when there's no one about, watch the sun come up on my last day.

Right, I goes, sure what time is it?

Tanya just shrugged. What does it matter, she says, throw something on, I'll cover my eyes.

I wasn't bothered if she saw me in the buff or not but I turned my back and put my aul blue shorts on. I was just pulling them up over my arse when she whistles. I looked back and she was peeking through her fingers and laughing. Aye, give us a break, I says, sure it's early and it's a bit cold in here. It wasn't cold at all, I was half asleep is all and I was talking shite.

We walked along the beach past all the huts right down to the end where you sometimes saw a couple of ancient Thai fellas fishing off the rocks. The sky was all purple and the sun was just starting to peek its wee head over the horizon. I hadn't seen the sunrise sober before in my life. It was dead quiet with only the sound of the waves sucking at the sand, no birds or nothing. Tanya sat down on the sand with her legs crossed like she was meditating or something but she was just staring out at the colours on the horizon with a smile on her face. She was fucking lovely at that moment, I'll always remember it, her face in profile against the rocks.

It's funny how the aul memory works. Sometimes that's all I 'member about a person is just one clear image, the rest all sort of blends together into more of a feeling than anything else. Maybe that's all you need is those photographs in the mind. When you're older, I suppose that's all you have. I've got loads of them already but they're not very nice most of them, I don't like thinking about it. It's all the bloody faces of Catholic lads I done over and worse. Don't even get me started on our Mark, I'm trying to block that out completely, those are not good memories to have.

Tanya stood up then and pulled her blouse off. She never wore a bra 'cos she had quite small wee breasts but I'd seen her wearing a bikini for going swimming. She had nothing on underneath this time. As she pulled the blouse off over her head I could see her hairy armpits. I'd seen them a couple of times by that stage and at first I was a bit disgusted but now I was sort of curious, it was a bit of a weird thing to see on a woman. I know it's natural and everything but I just wasn't used to it. No way the girls back home would ever not shave their pits. The fisherman pants were off next and there she was in the nuddy right next to me. She had a big hairy triangle between her legs too. I was a bit shocked at the sight of it even though I suspected she was like that as I'd seen wee hairs sticking out the side of her bikini bottoms when we'd been swimming. Without a word she walked down to the water and ran into the sea. The arms went up above her head and she dived into the waves. She had a big tattoo on her lower back, one of them tribal ones. It made my aul Loyalist ones look like shite.

There was something beautiful and free about our Tanya that I'd never seen in a woman before. It's like she was living in her own world and wasn't carrying around any aul hang-ups from the past. Everyone I knew was fucked up and I started to think maybe that was just home, maybe it didn't have to be like that.

I took the aul shorts off and ran into the sea as well. Tanya swam over, came up behind me and gave me a hug. I could feel her wee body pressing into the back of me. Her arms was round my chest and her chin was resting on my shoulder as the two of us watched the sun coming up over the ocean. There was still a wee bit of that phosphorescence stuff floating in the water, sure you could see it glowing whenever you kicked your feet or your hands.

I'll miss you, Tanya, I says, what am I going to do after you're away?

She plants a wee kiss on my neck. I could feel myself shaking but it was maybe just the cold water.

You'll have some other girl in your bed next week, she goes.

I haven't had you in my bed yet, I says.

You never asked, she goes, biting me on the shoulder all playful.

Is that all it would of took, me asking?

Hmm, she goes.

Right, I says, feeling like a right dumb cunt for not saying nothing before, well what are your plans for your last day?

Oh you know me, she says, I'm not much of a one for making plans.

Right, I goes, well can I make a wee suggestion?

Just a wee one then, she laughs. I knew she liked me saying wee.

I turned round in her arms then so I was facing her. She was a lot smaller than me and I could feel her fanny hair rubbing against my stomach under the water. Needless to say she was giving me the horn like nobody's business.

Come here and I'll whisper it in your ear, I says.

She turned her head so I could put my lips up close to her ear. The sea was turning a weird turquoise sort of colour.

What do you say we don't bother getting dressed the rest of the day?

A naked day, she whispers back into my ear.

Aye, we come back here tonight and swim in the same spot.

I wanted to put the lips on her real bad but she let go of me then and says, come on, if we want to avoid putting our clothes on we better run back along the beach before anyone wakes up and sees us.

That broke the wee romantic moment but it was a bit of fun getting back to shore and charging down the beach trying not to laugh and wondering if any early risers would see us. My aul knob was an early riser himself, sure I'd never run with a hard-on before but it went down soon enough. We went back to Tanya's hut and by that time I was getting used to walking around with nothing on but as soon as we were inside I couldn't stand it no more and I pulled her in to me and started snogging the face off of her.

Go easy, she says, your stubble's dead sharp, you'll give me pash rash.

What's that, I says.

She laughs then and goes, never mind, come to bed.

Music to my ears, I says.

And that's the way it was, all day. We must of done it six or seven times, I didn't think that was even possible. You hear stories that women who don't shave stink but it's not true, the smell of her was gorgeous, so it was, I was licking the sweat right off of her.

In between times when we were lying on the bed recovering she would pick up the guitar and sing me a wee song. I never heard the like of it. Some of them were hers and some of them were more famous ones but her own versions of them. She played this dead slow version of 'Girls Just Wanna Have Fun' that was brilliant, I nearly bawled, so I did. But the best was a song called 'Summertime'. Tanya says it was from some aul opera by Gershwin but her favourite version was by Ella Fitzgerald. I never heard of either of them but the way Tanya sung it naked sitting up on her knees with her head all bowed to one side, I could've died right there and then in that hut and my worthless fucking aul life would of been complete enough.

I still think about her sometimes. She pops into my head when I'm not expecting it and all of a sudden I'm back on that beach watching the sun come up or lying on her mattress in the hut, watching a wee bead of sweat running down her arm. Wherever I am fades away into the background and I feel an aul pang of regret as she leans down to me and goes, *Hush little baby, don't you cry*. I hope she's all right. Knowing our Tanya, she's probably sitting on some beach down in the Australia right now, singing her songs to some other fella, the two of them warm and happy and free.

Phi Phi was party central at the best of times and I threw myself into bed with loads of women and got into a few fights and that. I lost myself there for a while I don't mind telling you, I was more than a wee bit fucked up to be honest. I remember having this German girl with dreadlocks shacked up with me for a week. She wasn't that nice-looking and her English wasn't the best but I didn't care, I just wanted to fuck the aul hole off of her and forget who I was sort of thing.

The funny thing was the son of the family who owned the huts I was staying in was watching the whole time through the slats, but I was none the wiser. He was a right crack-up, the wee bastard, sure I liked him. I used to muck around with him on the beach, carry him on my shoulders and that and show him how to do choke-holds. I told him off when I heard he'd been watching me shagging all the women though. Sure I was out of it on Chang and Red Bull half the time and I don't think I was setting a very good example for the wee cunt, performance wise.

I done a bit of training with the barman Som and his pal. They'd both been in the army, sure they still have national service in Thailand, I couldn't believe it. Loads of countries still have it, I was amazed by that, sure they done away with it in the UK after the war. I met all these French and Swiss and Israelis who come through the Thailand and they'd all been in the army, some of them had to fight and that. Fucking mad, so it is.

Anyway, the Thai lads were dead fit, not an ounce of fat on the cunts, sure that's why all the backpacker girls went mad for them. Aul Som served drinks at the bar down on the beach, he was stoned out of his mind half the time but he told me one night he fucked about two hundred women a year.

Bollocks, I says, even I don't get through that many and sure I've got fuck-all else to do.

Serious, he goes, the western men all come to Thailand to pay for sex and the women come here to get it for free.

Fuck sake, I goes, that's sexual discrimination, so it is, sure you must spend a fortune on rubbers.

He looks at me all funny then and says, I don't understand, Billy.

Rubbers, I goes, flunkies, johnnies, you know?

Oh, he says, not really, only about half the women want me to, the rest don't say anything.

Are you fucking serious, I goes, sure what about the AIDS and the HIV, are you not worried about getting it?

He just shrugs like the possibility of it was so remote it wasn't worth thinking about. Jesus, I was thinking, he could have it already and be giving it to half the backpackers in the country, I better mind.

Him and his mate were good at the aul kickboxing. They showed me a couple of muaythai moves that were fucking deadly, so they were. You can paralyse someone easy if you hit them right on a certain spot on the spine. I was pretty good at the aul scrapping anyway from my younger days on the Shankill estate but I never learned nothing like this. After a couple of months training with those lads I was about ready to jump in the ring and knock the fuck out of some big cunt. The only problem is that knowing how to kill someone with your bare hands doesn't usually mix very well with the booze and feeling sorry for yourself. I was ready to snap, so I was. Lucky for me you can get away with just about anything in Thailand. It's not like the peelers are going to turn up in an aul jam sandwich and have you up in front of the magistrate for assault and battery. You can assault and batter people all you like, sure no one says nothing.

It was some English lads who copped it the worst from me. Honest to God, I don't know why we Prods bother aligning ourselves with England so much. The fucking Union Jack's hanging everywhere like we're dead patriotic or something. I know it's 'cos we want to remain part of the UK and tell everyone we're British and not Irish, but seriously once you meet a bunch of English lads on holidays it'd fucking put you off, so it would. Sure they're the worst, most annoying cunts out. They've got an aul chip on their shoulder or something, like just because they used to rule the world everyone's supposed to bow down to them and I don't like that, so I don't.

Sure have you ever been to England? What an aul shitehole. And yet they swan around like they're the best thing since sliced bread. It does my fucking head in. Every couple of days a bunch of them would come through Phi Phi and piss everyone off with all their shouting about En-ger-land and how they're going to win the next World Cup. They're fucking deluded, so they are. They can't handle the truth, like yer man Jack Nicholson says in that film.

So I was knocking about with this English girl, sure the women are far superior to the men over there, they're loads funnier and usually won't start a fight over nothing like they have to prove themselves and they're fucking good-looking too. She had lovely pale skin only she got sunburnt easy so she had to watch it. She was one of those frail English-rose types but she was all right, she was only on the island for five days and she calmed me down a bit with her quiet voice and sarcastic sense of humour.

Her name was Claire and she got me off the beach and onto one of those wee mopeds, driving round the island for a look. She sat behind me holding on with her delicate arms. She brought out the protective side of me, so she did. The roads were fucked on the island, all hilly and full of potholes, it was quite dangerous riding the motorbike if you didn't know what you were doing. Loads of the backpackers had taken a spill or burned themselves on the exhaust. We only crashed the once into the bushes and it was more funny than anything else.

We were relaxing by the bar one night, sure she got pished after a couple of drinks and would want to go back to the hut for a ride. I took it easy on her though, I didn't give her a good aul reaming like I did with some of them, sure I needed to calm down anyway, I was a bit pent up with tension or something. Turns out what I needed was just to knock the fuck out of someone and here comes the perfect candidates.

Som was obsessed with yon Chili Peppers album, *Blood Sugar Sex Magik*, I think he fancied himself as looking a bit like the lead singer. Loads of the Thai lads grew their hair long after they come out of the army. Anyway Som was playing it as usual and 'Under the Bridge' came on. Now there was a few English lads further down the bar, I had my eye on them 'cos they were a bit annoying and I was trying to have a wee laugh and a joke with Claire who'd sort of fallen for me. Course they're pished and start singing the lyrics dead loud, there was a bit of an edge to them like they were pissed off or something, typical fucking English lads in a group spoiling for a fight over nothing like I said before.

After the song was over one of the lads with an aul pinched face leans over the bar and starts shouting at Som to put on some Take That. Som just shakes his head no and the English lad starts abusing him, as do his mates. Put it on, you black cunt, they're saying. Som was outnumbered and he looks over at me 'cos he knows I hate that boy-band shite. I says, excuse me a wee minute Claire, I've just got a bit of business to attend to, you stay here out of the way love, I'll not be long.

Claire had the good sense just to nod and say, be careful, she knew what was coming and had seen me doing the muaythai on the beach so she knew I was going to burst them.

Youse are not putting that on, I goes to the English lad, that's music for wee girls. And that's a friend of mine youse are calling a black cunt, by the way.

The eyes lit up on the three of them but I could see straightaway the two at the back were shitting themselves at the muscles on me and all the Loyalist tattoos. The aul NO SURRENDER across the chest works wonders sometimes, so it does.

You got a problem, mate? the one with the pinched face goes.

Jesus, I was thinking, how come they always say that? It's right annoying, so it is. You worked that out all by yourself did you, I says, sure you must be the brains of the operation.

Fooking Paddies, all think you're fooking hilarious, he goes.

Aye, I says, sure that's why all your women go for us rather than ugly cunts like youse. Look at the wee puckered mouth on ye, sure I've seen better-looking rusty sheriff's badges.

You better shut it, you fooking Paddy cunt, he goes and stands up trying to look menacing or something.

I'd had enough of playing around, sure he'd no banter on him at all. There was only one thing for it so I grabbed him by the throat and lifted him up and bashed his head on the wooden beam of the low roof. He tried kicking me in the chest but he was only wearing sandals, it was pathetic so it was. One of them flew off and landed in the sink behind the bar. Som lifted it out with two fingers like it was a dead rat and threw it to the other two who were standing back all shocked.

Take it easy, mate, one of them shouts, thinking about coming forward.

Shut your gobs, I goes, or youse'll be next. I slammed the one with the pinched face down on the bar, sure his face was even more pinched after that. He was trying to scratch me with his long fingers so I grabbed his bollocks with my other hand and crushed them real hard. My name's not Paddy, I goes. I let him go then just to see if he'd drop it at that or if he was a fighter and all credit to him he come at me real furious like. I let him punch me a couple of times but he'd more spirit than experience 'cos he kept trying to hit me exactly the same way over and over.

Come on, Dave, get stuck into him, one of his mates

goes and I actually laughed.

Aye, come on, Dave, I says, you're such a big man, why don't you try and hit me like one. I fucking hate cunts called Dave, I don't know why, I just never met one I liked. It's funny how you get hung up on wee things like that. Anyway I could see Claire holding her hands over her mouth looking a bit upset, I wondered what was wrong with her, then I realised I was just standing there letting this piss-weak English cunt punch me in the head and I wasn't doing nothing. Sure I could hardly feel it anyway, I was just killing time hoping maybe his pals would join in so's I could get a proper fight but they were too feared.

Come on, Billy, Claire squeals and by the sound of her voice I realised she was worried about me, she thought I was taking a beating. That pushed me over the edge then and I snapped out of it. I laid into the three of them big time, sure they didn't stand a chance. I put the back of my hand across Dave's face, swatting him like a fly sort of thing, he never saw it coming and fell back against the bar. Som darted in to lift a glass out of the way not so's Dave wouldn't hurt himself just so's it wouldn't get broke, it was quite comical watching him in the background, he'd seen it a thousand times before I suppose like all barmen.

I stepped up to the other two then and for a laugh grabbed their heads to bash them together. I thought that would be dead funny except it was a bit cocky of me and the one on the left wriggled free and spun round to jump on my back. Even though he was a bit of a fat fuck he moved fast so he did and the weight of him on me was something fierce, he must of been shovelling the aul green curry in like nobody's business. Anyway he started clawing at my eyes from behind, fuck he near blinded me I was so preoccupied trying to shuck him off of me that his pal had a free go to start laying into me from the front. When your blood's up sure you can't feel nothing, he could of been stabbing me with an aul broken bottle for all I knew. I put one big paw on his chest and shoved him away dead hard, he staggered back and fell over one of the stools and cracked his head on the way down, probably a concussion I was thinking, good that'll learn ye.

Yer man Dave came charging back then and I windmilled round, he kicked me one in the thigh sort of karate-style, I think he was aiming for my balls. Good job he missed, that would only of pissed me off even more. Fuck that I was thinking, I'll show ye some proper moves. I squatted down a bit and tensed the aul leg muscles then threw the fat fucker on my back right over my shoulder, it was amazing actually I'd not thrown someone like that for ages, never a fella as big anyway. You should of seen the shock on his face as he went over, if I hadn't of been so busy I'd of laughed. He sort of half landed on Dave, not like in the movies, a bit messy like these things always are in real life.

I was fed up by then, my Claire was squealing like she wanted to step in and help me by smashing a pot plant over one of their heads or something, course there wasn't any geraniums to hand and I raised a finger to warn her off, if one of them had of slapped her or something sure it would be the last thing he done. The fat one kicked me in the shins from the ground and the other one not Dave had gathered himself up and was trying to rugby tackle me to get me down.

I lost the bap then, fuck they were dead annoying, I balled up my fists and started in with the muaythai on them like I'd learned and the aul red mist came down over me. I can't even 'member what I done to them, all I know is next thing Som was pulling me back shouting that's enough, Billy, you're going to kill them. I calmed down quick as fuck after that like nothing had even happened, walked back to where I was sitting and took a wee sip of my drink. Our Claire was even paler than usual. I winked at her and says, are you all right.

Never mind me, she goes, what about you?

No bother, I goes, sure it's all in a night's work.

You're not even shaking or anything, Claire says.

I held my hand out and right enough it was rock solid, I hardly even had an aul adrenaline rush or nothing. I glanced down at the floor of the bar where the three English cunts were lying and I says to her, hold on a minute, one last thing.

Billy, she goes, I think they've had enough.

Aye, I know, I says, it's just a wee something to make them think twice in future, sure you have to teach them a lesson otherwise they'll never learn, lads like that.

I kneeled down and bent the little finger back on the right hand of each of them until it broke at the knuckle. It was a bit nasty but that was one of my trademarks from back home. Claire didn't even turn away, she only grimaced a wee bit, I was quite surprised and I started thinking that maybe I'd underestimated her, she was maybe tougher than I'd given her credit for and here was me treating her like she was a piece of fine china in a museum or something.

We had a brilliant aul ride that night, she thought I was the bee's knees after that. I was a bit sore in places where the English had hit me, didn't feel it at the time of course but there was a couple of big bruises on my arms and back and a purple one forming on my leg where one of those twats kicked me with his aul pointy toes, probably hurt himself more. Claire ran her fingertips over them, her nails was dead short sure you can't hardly keep good nails clean in the Thailand when you're bumming around the beach and that. She traced the outlines like they were wee islands on a map and it was quite nice so it was just feeling the gentle touch of a woman after all that aul scrapping. Once in a while she pressed in on a bruise and I jumped and goes fuck sake you're hurting me more than they did, she liked that but then she'd kiss me on the bruise and I'd forgive her.

It was funny seeing her long pale body crawling like an explorer over my aul tan hide, it made me dead rampant, but when I tried to roll her over she'd bite her lip and hold me down. I let her, knowing it was making her wet. She found a couple of aul scars I'd forgotten about from when I was in a fight outside a pub and fell on some broken glass. She asked how I got them and I told her but then she asked about the big one down my side and I just said it was a long story. We've got all night, she goes.

Aye, I says, but I've got other plans.

Your tattoos are wild, she goes, pretty scary.

I didn't say nothing, what can you say to that anyway?

She draped herself on me and was lying all quiet with her head on my chest when out of the blue she goes, you'd never let anyone hurt me, would you, Billy?

Love, I says, if any man laid a finger on you sure they'd be digging his bones up out of the desert in fifty years wondering who the fuck he was.

She goes, I've never felt so safe in my life.

No idea what happened to the English cunts. Last I saw them they were limping off crying to get First Aids, that's not me being funny by the way that's what it actually says on the sign, the Thais are a right crack-up so they are. Suppose they fucked off back to where they come from after that to talk about what big men they were and how brilliant Paul Gascoigne was and how they were going to win the next World Cup or something. Aye, sure good luck with that, you bunch of eejits.

Usually I wouldn't mind giving lads like that a hiding, sure they deserved it so they did and I done much worse before, but I didn't feel the best after to be honest. It wasn't the aul bruises, they always fade, there was just something about the whole atmosphere of the place that was starting to get me down. Maybe it was that I knew Claire wouldn't hang around. Even though she liked me, after a wee while she'd be away on a plane just like the lads I'd given a beating to. They sort of win in the end 'cos it's just an aul holiday for them, just an adventure that'll turn into stories to tell their pals. They get to go home whereas me, Loyalist hard man, big fucking whoop, sure I'm stuck so I am.

Phuket. Now there's a place that's well named. I went out about eleven to get some breakfast to soak up the booze. Lo and behold who should I see at the café down the road but these two blonde bints I'd clocked the day before. They looked bored as fuck but they were both already pretty tan. Not as dark as me, mind, but still not bad. I suppose they had fuck all else to do but lie on the beach. The older German men didn't seem to like them being around, like they were seeing something they shouldn't. Probably reminded them of their daughters. Their faces perked up at the sight of me so I went over to sit with them.

Bout ye ladies, I says. Youse picked a right spot for the holidays. They looked at each other funny and for a minute I thought fucking hell some of these aul German cunts *have* brought their daughters with them, the sick bastards. Then one of them goes to me in perfect English, we didn't know it was this bad, she says, we've only got a few days leave from work, we were staying in Malaysia but it was too weird. She had a strange accent. I could tell she was European but there was a bit of an American twang in there. Then the other one goes, this is just as bad, you're the only young person we've seen, what are you doing in a place like this?

I ordered fried rice with an egg on top in the local lingo. I could see they were impressed but obviously I wasn't going to tell them the truth of the matter so I says, same as youse, I heard the craic was good here but looks like we were misinformed, aye? Fucking sick, so it is, what do youse think?

They nodded. I could tell they were relieved I wasn't a sex tourist like all the aul fellas but at the same time I was thinking I'd better get out of there pronto before one of the wee tan whores came along and says hello, Billy, how's the rash, sorry about that by the way.

Don't tell us youse two are German, I goes.

Nah, no way, the first one says with a look like she was chewing on a lemon. We're Dutch. We work for KLM and we got free flights out here, we wanted to go somewhere nice and tropical but we'll know better next time. Are you Scottish?

I get that all the time. Most cunts can't tell the fucking difference but at least she asked rather than going what part of Scotland are you from. Nah, I says, I'm Irish.

That was playing it safe. She didn't press it like most do and ask what part. I usually say Leitrim anyway, as no cunt's heard of that. Sure I couldn't even tell you where it was myself, like.

I love the Irish accent says the other one, whose hair was a bit darker and shorter than the first one though they looked pretty much the same in the face. The first one had bigger tits. I could hardly take my eyes off them the whole time but the second one had nipples you could hang your coat on. Since I'd sat down they'd been straining against her blue bikini top. They were both wearing sarongs around their bottom halves and expensive sunglasses. D&G on the both of them, probably got them cheap in the duty free working for the airline and all.

Aye? I says, sure youse have got lovely accents yourselves. Your English is cracker, so it is. How much longer are youse staying?

We're flying back down to KL tomorrow night, the first one goes. What a dump. The men down there are horrible.

Aye, I says, two gorgeous blonds like youse, I suppose you got a bit of hassle from the local lads.

It was unbelievable, the second one says, folding her big lips around the straw of her drink and looking at me over her glasses.

I felt a twitch in my shorts and pulled my chair in closer to the table.

Everywhere we went we'd get followed and well, other stuff too, you know.

She looked a bit embarrassed as she said this but I reckoned it was all for show.

The first one laughs and says, on our first day we bought some food from the hawker's market and sat in the park. Then this guy just walked up and opened his zip and started masturbating in front of us.

You're kidding me on, I says.

Seriously, she goes, he just stood there staring at us while he was doing it. We didn't know what to do.

Put you off your laksa, I suppose.

She laughed quite loud and the second one started snickering too. Yeah! she says.

So what did youse do? Call the peelers?

We told him to fuck off and leave us alone but he just ignored us so we packed up to leave but by the time we did that he, you know, finished.

Did no one else see or say anything?

No! she goes, there were other people in the park too but he had his back to them. Can you believe it?

Fucking wild. Dirty bastard.

You're not going to believe the next bit, the second one says, all flushed in the cheeks. This has happened to us five times so far on this holiday. Everywhere we go there's men in the bushes or standing around playing with themselves.

Look on the bright side, I says, at least youse are getting plenty of attention from the fellas.

God, we wish, goes the second one and then the first one scolds her with her eyes. I mean, we wouldn't mind having some fun on this trip, I just don't want to see cum spurting everywhere when I'm trying to eat a sandwich.

I thought that was funny as fuck and started laughing dead loud. Aye, right enough, I goes, hold the mayo please.

They looked at each other all wide eyes and burst out laughing. The first one touched me on the arm and says, thank God to meet someone normal for a change.

Aye, the place is full of weirdoes, I says, trying not to think of the ping-pong ball landing in my pint of Stella the night before. I'm getting out of here myself in a couple of days.

As soon as the words were out of my mouth I knew it was the truth. I'd had enough of Phuket already, even though I'd not been here more than a few weeks. It was time to move on and find somewhere else to shack up for a while, maybe mix it up with some good-looking young ones like these two honeys.

The second one was giving the first one the stares like she was trying to tell her something. The first one chewed on her bottom lip like she was making some big decision. I pretended to be oblivious and ate my rice. The first one let out a big sigh and said something to her mate in Dutch. I could tell it was a question from the way the other one answered all firm like. Obviously you don't have to be a rocket scientist to work out it was me they were discussing.

I never let on and broke the fried egg up into the rice. The first one protested a bit and then the other one nodded, rolled her eyes and made some concession. They both laughed a bit dirty then. Even though I couldn't speak the Dutch, it was clear as fuck they were working out which one was going to get her jollies with me. Argue all you like ladies, I was thinking, this is a win-win situation for me, though it didn't seem right that one of them should lose out. Fuck, I thought, if only Mark was here, he could of been my wingman. Then I 'membered about him and that put me in a bad mood for a wee minute.

We've got a hire car, the first one says, and we thought we'd drive around to one of the resorts and use their beach for a change. We heard if you walk round the rocks it's a bit more private. Do you want to come with us?

Sure, sounds good, I says, all casual like, though I was thinking private? You fucking beauty. If youse want to go and get ready, I'll meet you back here in half an hour or something. I'm Billy, by the way.

They told me their names was Eva and Katelijn, though I had to get the one with the big nips to spell hers out for me. I could tell she liked hearing me say it. I waited until they were out of sight and then wolfed down the rest of the fried rice. I ran back to the room and had a shower, made sure my bollocks were shaved and my pubes were under control. I took a dump and shaved my face and all so's I'd be ready for them. I slipped a couple of flunkies into the wee pocket on my swimming trunks and grabbed my towel. It wasn't very clean but what can you do, sure it was just for lying on anyway.

I had a couple of pairs of aul sunglasses that I'd bought

at the market in Bangkok. I chose the Ray-Bans, they were the best ones. They were all fakes of course but they were dead cheap and who can tell the fucking difference anyway like? I threw on a short-sleeved white shirt, it looked beezer with the aul tan and covered up my tattoos so's I wouldn't scare the shite out of them. There was no mirror in the place but I felt pretty good, like I was yer man Pierce Brosnan or something, even though he's a Fenian and in some soft shite movies.

The girls were waiting for me back at the café. They'd both changed their bikinis. Katelijn was wearing a lime-green number that looked cracker on her, so it did. Eva had on a black one. Blondes can't usually get away with that but she was so tan it looked fucking amazing. Her tits were bulging out of it and I was glad she was driving so I couldn't see her that well.

I sat in the back and Katelijn kept turning round for a banter as we were going across the island. It was slow going as there was so many of those wee mopeds the Thais all seem to love. We saw one where the fucker had his wife and three kids on the cunt. His wee baby was balancing between the handlebars. They didn't have no helmets on or nothing. It's a fucking mad place, so it is. The peelers'd pull you over in five minutes for that back home. The girls weren't that fussed, like. Katelijn says they do the same thing on bikes back in Rotterdam.

Is that right, I says, sure youse are mad and all.

Yeah! she goes, we are a bit mad. She was getting herself all worked up, I think she was just nervous or something. They must not have talked to a man in ages so I played it cool and pretended to like the music they were playing on the aul stereo. It was that Europop shite that you have to be pished to dance to. Anyone who's ever done eccies in a good club hates that bollocks but I could've listened to Celine Dion if I thought Katelijn was going to open her legs for me.

Anyway we stopped in the car park of some fancy resort and wandered down to the beach. I thought we'd have to pay or someone would ask us what we were doing or something but there was no staff around, just a few families with blotchy sunburns. We walked right past them down the beach to the rocks. It was a bit dodgy climbing over them in sandals so I told the girls to take their shoes off and just watch where they were stepping. I led the way and they followed me until we came to this gap in the rocks where the sea was coming in. It wasn't that wide but when Katelijn saw it she goes, shit we can't go any further.

What are you talking about, I says, sure we can jump over that.

I don't know, she says, it looks a bit far.

Bollocks, I goes, and takes a run at it. Sure I jumped right over and landed easy on the other side. Throw us the bags over, I goes, and they did. Eva jumped over after me no problem like, she wasn't bothered at all. Katelijn was a bit scared, she didn't have as long legs as her pal.

Sure I'll catch you, I says, jump straight for me, just

don't trip or nothing. She was worried about nothing in the end, she made it across no bother at all but she reached out for my arms anyway and I pulled her in close so she could see how strong I was. Eva rolled her eyes and walks away smiling. She said something in the Dutch and Katelijn went all red it was probably why don't you just suck his aul knob right here, love.

I laughed and says c'mon.

The wee beach was private enough. By the time we climbed down from the rocks it was another ten minutes so if anyone else tried to follow us we'd see them coming a mile off. It was fucking lovely, so it was. There was a rocky slope up behind the beach and no way round the rocks on the other side so this was the end of the line. The girls thought it was brilliant, I think they'd been looking for a beach to themselves their whole holiday. Sure you always hear the backpackers going on about that. It's like the ultimate luxury or something, a beach with no other cunt sweating their arse off on it. Normally I couldn't give a fuck like, but when the Dutch girls started laying their towels out and taking their sarongs off, I could see the sense in it.

I threw my aul manky towel down next to theirs and took my shirt off. When the girls were busy taking stuff out of their wee beach bag I slipped the two flunkies out of my trunks and wrapped them up in my shirt for safekeeping. I brought two even though it was pretty obvious I was going to hump Katelijn. You never know, I thought, maybe Eva will want in on the action but she might want her own condom 'cos some girls are funny about that.

When I looked around again I couldn't believe it. They were both topless and rubbing suntan lotion into their tits. I started to get a stiff one straightway and had to angle my leg to try and hide it. Eva's tits were those big full and heavy kind with the huge brown circles behind the nipples. They were dead tan but looked better when she was sitting up. When she lay down they sort of spread out towards her armpits. They must have been soft and doughy. Katelijn's were smaller but fucking gorgeous. They looked dead firm and she was all red in the face from rubbing the suntan lotion on her nipples, which were about half the size of my little finger I swear to God. They must of both been going topless the whole time on their trip 'cos their nips weren't pink at all, they'd gone dark brown from the sun.

We all lay there for a bit and I had to roll over onto my stomach to hide the bulge in my trunks, there wasn't much room in there for the aul fella. Katelijn's bikini was one of those ones with just a patch of material at the front and the back, tied together at the sides by two wee pieces of string. Eva was lying between the two of us so I couldn't see her all that well and had to keep sitting up, pretending to stare out to sea or something but squinting to get a gander out the side of my sunglasses.

Youse two have got nice tans, I says, trying to make conversation and thinking what a load of aul shite.

Yeah thanks, Katelijn goes, but they're not all over.

Every time I'm in the shower I see this white triangle staring up at me and think it's stupid.

Sure I'm the same, I says, and pulls down the side of my trunks to show them the white band on my skin, the aul knob had calmed himself by this stage. It was a bit flirtatious but I actually agreed with her. It was dumb as fuck being tan all over except round your bollocks and that. As if that part of a man doesn't look stupid enough.

Oh good, she goes, so you don't mind if I go naked?

Stupidest fucking question I ever heard, like.

Aye, go ahead, I says, acting like my heart wasn't pumping in my chest, doesn't bother me like.

I tried my best not to watch with my tongue hanging out as she untied the bikini at both sides and pulled it out from under her. She smiled at me as if she was saying what do you fucking think of that then, boyo. Fuck me, I could feel my knob pulsing in my shorts, it was like let me at her for fuck sake. She had a wee strip of blonde hair down there that stopped just above her slit, which you could just see the top of. Christ, it was the most gorgeous fucking sight in the world. I had to lie down so I couldn't see it, even though I could hear the wee thing calling to me.

After a bit Katelijn sat up and said she was going for a swim and did we want to come in with her. Eva just shook her head and I goes, aye in a minute, as I was trying to name all the football teams in the First and Second Divisions just to get my knob to go down. It didn't help watching her walk down to the water's edge all naked and that. She was fit as fuck.

Once she was in the sea I started to calm down as all I could see was her head. Satisfied that the big fella downstairs was in a fit state to be seen in public, I pulled my trunks off and sat up on my knees. I still had a bit of a semi but it was on the way down rather than on the way up. Still, I could feel Eva copping an eyeful from under her sunglasses.

Your ass *is* white, she laughed.

I wiggled it for her and she laughed a bit more. You coming in for a dip, I says.

Nah, she goes, I'll wait until you two get back.

Fair enough, I goes, wondering what she had under her own bikini bottoms.

I padded down to the water, feeling a bit weird walking naked on the beach. I waded in until the sea lapped at my balls. Katelijn swam over and stood up, droplets flying off her hair and tits.

It's cold but you have to plunge right in, she says, eyes all wide and excited at the sight of me standing there in the buff, my cock flopping against my leg and still a bit bigger than normal. I'm not a bad aul swimmer so I dived forward into the next wave it was quite refreshing actually. I've no bother opening my eyes under the water too though most people need goggles and that. It was shallow and I could see the bottom dead easy. There was loads of wee fish darting about doing their business.

I could see Katelijn's legs so I headed towards her and grabbed her ankle just messing around like. I popped up out of the water right in front of her and she squealed but next thing you know she had her arms around my neck and was pushing up against me. She put the lips on me then and I gave her a good aul snog, she tasted all salty from the water but it was all right so it was, her tongue flicked in and out of my mouth like one of those wee fish.

I'd never done it in the sea before, I wasn't even sure you could as the waves kept knocking us about. I could feel Katelijn's nips poking me in the chest like a couple of wasps trying to get out of a jam jar so I grabbed her tits and rolled her nips in my fingers. She pressed her mouth into me even harder for a minute then broke away and splashed back in the water.

You're keen, I says, trying to grab her again.

I need sex really badly right now, she goes.

Aye, well you've come to the right place, I says, sure I'll sort you out no problem.

God, you're the sexiest man I've seen in ages, she goes.

Well thanks very much, I says, but that's not saying much if the only other men you've seen lately were those wankers in the park.

Can I tell you something, she says all quiet, promise you won't say anything to Eva.

Course, I goes, sure what is it, don't tell us you used to be a man or something.

No, nothing like that, she says, God those men they were really unattractive and everything, I mean I'd never go with any of them but it actually really turned me on seeing them do that. Just the idea that as soon as they saw me it made them so horny they had to masturbate straightaway, there's something incredibly sexy about it.

Aye, well I started to get hard as soon as I sat down next to you at breakfast this morning, I says to her, sure you must have that effect on men all the time.

She liked that and she goes, are you hard right now, Billy?

Course I am, I says, sure I only have to look at you, you're a fucking beautiful woman, what man wouldn't go mad for you?

She swum back over to me then and gave me a wee kiss on the lips but not too much like. She had one hand around my neck and was looking into my eyes all sort of dreamy when she put her other hand around my knob under the water and started stroking it. I kept trying to put the lips on her but she'd pull back, she just wanted to watch the expression on my face while she rubbed my cock. It was just getting good when she let go and swam away, laughing all evil.

Where you going, I says, back to the beach to see if I can get my white bits tan, she goes. Aye right, brilliant, I says, I'll be there in a minute. She had me all rampant, sure I was ready to bend her over solid but it was a bit funny with Eva being there and all, sure she hadn't said much and I didn't want to jinx the whole thing. So I waited for a bit and did a bit of swimming to try and take my mind off of her. Eventually the aul knob went down again. I felt sorry for him, he was up and down like a fucking yo-yo but I didn't mind so much 'cos I knew sometimes when that happens and you finally do get your rocks off it's a fucking good one.

I started to get cold so I went back in, striding up the sand balls to the wind like I couldn't give a fuck who saw me. It was pretty good actually, I could go for the aul nudist beach after all. Katelijn was lying on her front wearing nothing but her sunglasses. Her legs was open a wee bit and I could see her fanny lips but it didn't bother me none, I just flopped down on my towel and put my Ray-Bans on like this was something I did every day. Sure you've seen one you've seen them all pretty much, even though they're all a wee bit different. It's not like she had something extra other women didn't have, though I knew I'd be investigating up close pretty fucking sharpish like.

Eva says something in the Dutch and gets up then to go for a swim. She still had her bikini bottoms on. Her arse had a bit of a wobble to it but she was all woman, you know. Anyway, she dives into the waves and starts powering out really far until she reaches the calm water and then just floats on her back sure she had plenty to keep her up, like my da used to say she's got a great set of lungs on her.

Me and Katelijn wasted no time after that. She rolled over onto her back and spread her legs so's I could see everything. I couldn't tell if she was wet from the sea or from the excitement of it all but I dived in straightaway. I reaches into my shirt for the flunky and tears it open.

Oh, you just made my day, Katelijn goes. She positions

herself on all fours on her towel, arse in the air and puts two fingers between her legs to spread her sticky wee fanny lips open for me. Fuck me really hard, she says. Aye, can do, I goes, brace yourself love, here I come.

She was so wet that I could hardly feel nothing. I was ramming her for ages and she was fucking loving it. The sweat was pouring down my back, so it was. She had a wee bit of downy blonde hair on her lower back too and that was all glistening with sweat. It was fucking hot work doing it out in the sun and I was thinking fuck me I wouldn't mind a wee swim after this, that'd be nice so it would. Beads of sweat were dripping down her back and running down over her arsehole so I stuck my middle finger in there and that was good so it was 'cos she clenched her fanny real tight then and dug her fingers into the sand.

I was going great guns but I had no feeling like I was going to come anytime soon and even though it was brilliant and I shouldn't complain my mind started to wander. I was thinking, where am I going to go after I fuck off out of here, maybe head east or something, there's a couple of nice wee islands you can get to from there, though what's the point. It would just be more of the same aul hole and Chang probably.

It struck me then as I was pumping away that I was bored as fuck of all this. What a thing to go through your head at a moment like that, sure I never thought I'd see the day but I couldn't deny I was restless with just wandering around the Thailand. I didn't like thinking about it but I knew I was a bit lost, I could hardly concentrate on what I was doing. I was carrying the aul Troubles with me and it was only a matter of time before I had to sort myself out, one way or the other.

Sure it wasn't really a moment for reflection though, not when there's a Dutch honey squirming away underneath ye gasping and clawing at the sand. She starts giving it the aul yes yes yes *ja ja ja* and saying something else in the Dutch too *ohhh dat ongelooflijk*, you didn't have to be an interpreter to work out she was getting her jollies and it done the job for me too, I just threw my head back and let it go.

There I was my aul knob pulsing away, Katelijn making these little satisfied yelps and who should I spot standing off to one side watching us but Eva. Sure I'd forgot all about her. Her head was cocked to one side like she was studying some strange animals in a nature documentary or something.

Nice sunglasses, she says to me, stepping out of her bikini bottoms.

It's easy to forget the Thais are Buddhists, most of them are anyway, sure I nearly died when the barman tells me what year it was. Here's me thinking it was 1996 but nah, he goes, it's 2539 in our calendar. I didn't know what the fuck he was on about at first but then he says to me, he says the Thailand is 543 years ahead of you.

How's that, I goes, are youse in the future or something, sure where's all your jetpacks and that? I couldn't make no sense of it, sure I just assumed the whole world had the same system. It blew me away, so it did.

When the Thai New Year came up this wee lad helped me and whoever else was staying in the huts to make these wee boat things out of sticks and mud. At midnight you lit a candle and stuck it in your boat, they were only about the size of your hand. Then you had to write down on tiny bits of paper all the things that were bothering you during the past year and that you wanted rid of out of your life. You burned them over the candle and threw the ashes into your boat and went down to the ocean and sent it out into the waves.

It was fucking magic so it was, there were hundreds of wee boats with candles in them drifting out on the water all along the beach where people were doing it. I suppose there was millions of them all around the country. I'd never seen the like of it and it's a fucking brilliant idea too, getting rid of all your aul problems even if it was just ceremonial or whatever.

I was dead pleased with my boat but when I put it in the water it only went out about five feet or something and then a wave comes in and swamps it. The cunt floated right back to my feet. I looked around and everyone else's was heading out to sea and I thought fuck me, that's just my luck so it is, saddled with the same aul fucking problems for another year.

I was getting restless anyway and I was thinking of taking the bull by the horns and fucking off somewhere else for a while even though my options were limited, so they were. After New Year I borrowed one of the aul mopeds and scooted up to the port where they had a couple of shops and a phone line. Sure I needed some more flunkies anyway, just in case mind. I gave Big Jim back home a call just to check in sort of thing and let him know I'd be moving on, he couldn't really talk, I think he had someone in the office with him and had to watch what he was saying but he gives me a number to write down.

You 'member Olly, he goes, sure he's down your way youse two should meet up or something.

The Frenchman who ran all that gear across to Marseille for us, I says, aye the very one Big Jim says, drop him a line Billy, here I'll have to go but give us a ring next month, you all right for money and that.

I told him I was and said cheerio then went and treated myself to a Mars Bar at the wee shop sure they're like hen's teeth and they charge you a fortune for them 'cos they know all the westerners are dying for a hit of chocolate and it's not like you can run round to the Spar when you're on some fucking aul island in the middle of the Andaman Sea.

Olly was this mad French cunt who was an officer in their army and he done us loads of favours, I 'membered him so I did, he was all right even though he was a Fenian, so were all the French but when it came to making money he was a smart one and didn't mind doing business with us Prods. He was in charge of transport or something and always had these wee convoys of trucks scooting about Europe and knew everyone so he did. If we wanted to get drugs or guns or anything dodgy in the slightest from A to B he was our man.

He was only a young lad like twenty or something, he was doing his national service, most of the young ones get it over with and then fuck off out of it but he stayed on and signed up for a couple more years 'cos he was making so much money and didn't have to pay for nothing, he had his own digs on some army base down near Lyon. I jawed on the phone with him a couple a times sure his English was brilliant so it was and he was dead funny I 'membered.

Why he was down my way, whatever that meant 'cos for all I knew he could be thousands of miles away in the Philippines or something, I could only imagine. He was probably on the run like me I was thinking and it might be all right meeting up with him 'cos sure he always had something going on at least I'd be guaranteed a fucking good time and some company with someone who knew the score, like.

It was a bit awkward getting in touch with the fucker sure I had to leave a couple of messages and run back and forth to the phone every day for a week but eventually I got a hold of him and he was chuffed to hear from me, turns out he was in sort of the same predicament I was. He'd done a runner from France with eighty grand in his aul skyrocket and was just knocking around like a beach bum trying to make it last 'cos he was feared to go back. Sure enough he'd been in the Philippines for ages but now he was next door to me down in Malaysia.

He said he'd been running a bit of resin in Penang but he didn't trust no one and sure it was the death penalty if you got caught so someone shopping you to the peelers was pretty fucking serious and he was dead paranoid.

I told him I was bored as fuck and he says, let's meet in the middle and check into the cheapest place you can find on Langkawi I hear it's nice there, plenty of rich women, except he says it in his French accent so instead of the and there he says ze and zere, you get the picture.

I was glad to be on the move actually so I caught the bus down to Satun pronto like. The ferry over to Langkawi was a bit fancy and there was loads of aul couples on it, I was thinking what the fuck does Olly want to meet up here for but I assumed he was taking the back door out of Penang probably to avoid paying someone, it wouldn't of surprised me with that cunt.

There was only one cheap joint on Langkawi, sure it was all resorts and that not the sort of place for the likes of me who was used to aul fleapits and shacks half falling into the sea. It wasn't even that cheap, to be honest I baulked a bit at handing the money over, I know I've got loads but you never know when you need a bit of stake money for a wee job or when you have to buy your way out of a fucking tight corner. The room was no great shakes but there was a lounge for hanging out in, it was all right actually 'cos the only people staying there were your real independent traveller types, sure you could tell straightaway from the state of them and none of them planned to stay long they were just ticking the island off some list in their Lonely Planet.

Some aul Scottish fella was arguing with a sunburnt English bint about India. She said it was shite and he was pissed off because he'd spent a couple of years there and she'd only been for a fortnight but still, she wouldn't back down. I could see him eyeballing my tatts and nodding so I guessed he was a Prod for he starts glaring at me for support.

Don't be looking at me I says to him, sure the closest I ever got to the India was down the takeaway on Chichester Street. Fucking beef madras went through me like a dose of salts, so it did.

The girl laughed, Japanese flag she goes.

What's that supposed to mean, I says.

You know, she goes, white with a red hole in the middle.

Oh aye, right enough, I goes, laughing a wee bit but thinking fuck sake what sort of thing is that for a woman to say to a man she's just met, not exactly the romantic type, are you love? I'm sure I was no oil painting myself but both her and the aul fella looked like they could do with a good going over with a scrubbing brush. Sure they had a layer of grime on them. Such is the way of it when you're travelling on a budget, I suppose.

I had to sit there for two days listening to their bickering and carrying on, they didn't even know each other and even though there was forty years between them sure you'd swear they were married or something. I told them to shut their gobs I don't know how many times but they didn't pay me no mind. The aul fella worried me a bit. He'd worked all over the world doing wee jobs here and there, saving enough to move on somewhere else. He reckoned he'd had a fantastic life and I wasn't doubting it but he looked about a hundred years old, sure his skin was like a prune or something.

I was thinking fuck me am I looking at myself in thirty years time, fuck I hope not, I better get myself sorted out before I end up like this aul cunt. The English girl had a right ugly face on her and a fair aul jiggle round the belly, she did nothing for me especially when she put her feet up on the table and started picking at her dirty toenails. She gave me a look sometimes like she wouldn't have minded a ride but there was no way I was going there. I couldn't wait for Olly to turn up 'cos I knew he'd fuck the arse off of her, sure he'd do anything with a pulse.

Took the cunt long enough getting there but I was glad to see him all the same. He just walks in one day like he'd lived there for years, some fellas have got a talent for that.

Billy Montgomery, he shouts, fucking hell look at you man.

Lieutenant Olivier Morel, I goes to him, where've you been, soldier.

He gave me a big hug and kissed me on both cheeks which surprised me a wee bit before I 'membered that these French cunts will kiss everyone that's just the way they are.

Who's this beautiful lady he goes, and the English girl went beetroot. I fucking knew it, so I did. I don't know why he bothered with half the women, he wasn't a bad-looking fella, dead tan like me of course from bumming around on the beaches except he had curly blond hair and wore wee round glasses. He had a permanent sweaty kind of look and this cheeky aul grin like where's the party at, let's go out and start some trouble, sort of thing. It was hard not to like him. It's no wonder he was into a bit of smuggling and adventuring and what have you. You couldn't imagine a fella like that sitting behind a desk in an aul fucking office.

Even though it was only lunchtime when he arrived we started hitting the cocktails, though I could see he was watching his money the same as me. He sat with his arm draped around my shoulders for a while and the English girl asked him loads of questions and he told her loads of lies that I backed him up on. I wasn't used to a man being in such close proximity to me but the French are different to the boring aul uptight fucking Brits. If any of the lads from the Shankill walked in and saw me sitting all cosy like with this blond Frenchman they'd be thinking we were bum chums or something.

The only man familiar with me was our Mark and we were brothers like so that was all right. I told Olly that one night a few weeks later and he just shrugged like it was nothing at all and says in France all men are brothers. That cut me up, so it did. The Brits are always slagging the French but as I found out they actually do loads of things better. *Liberté égalité fraternité* was their motto Olly explained to me, freedom equality brotherhood. And they fucking took it seriously and all. Our ones wouldn't even know the meaning of words like that, me least of all. Sure I was the last one to understand brotherhood.

It only took him a few hours to get invited up to

that ugly bitch's room, it disgusted me the thought of her aul dirty feet with the big black hairs sticking out of the toes but Olly wasn't as fussy as me, for years the only women he'd seen were on posters stuck up on the inside of lockers so fair enough and at least the English girl was getting her end away at last, maybe then she'd shut her gob for a while.

We never hung round long enough to find out. Olly crept into the room early the next morning and says to me, grab your shit we're getting out of here, you didn't pay the bar bill last night did you?

Course not, I says, what do you take me for?

Right, come on then, he goes.

Fuck sake, I says, it must be about four in the morning.

There's a ferry at six, he goes, let's make sure we're on it. This is our Olly all over, I was thinking.

We were looking over our shoulders the whole time before the ferry left just in case a bunch of Malays with machetes turned up looking for the money we owed them, or even worse the English girl.

How was she, I asked Olly, a good ride?

All right I suppose, he goes, she smelled weird.

Hope you didn't suck on her aul hairy toes, I says.

Olly laughs then and goes, yes! They were hairy weren't they but don't worry I kept well away from them, how come you didn't fuck her?

Sure she was disgusting, I says, no offence like.

What do you mean, he goes, looking a bit hurt.

Well let's just say she wasn't my type, I says, I'm into

the whatchamacallit intellectual types these days, the ones that take care of themselves and have a good head on them.

You get many of them round these parts, he goes, laughing.

I suppose not, I says, but the life we have puts you out of touch with what's going on, there's no way to learn nothing unless in books and I get fed up with that, do you not?

C'est vrai, he goes, which means right enough in our lingo, that's why I was dealing in Penang just to keep myself from going crazy and feel like I was doing something.

Aye, it sounds mad though. Were you not feared of getting caught, sure they're dead strict and that.

Well I'm out of it now, he says, but if you're interested I've got the number of a guy up in Bangkok who's looking for westerners, it's easy money and low risk.

What is it, I says, mule work, 'cos call me mad but I don't fancy swallowing twenty flunkies full of horse. One of them bursts and you're proper fucked.

No no, he says, no way nothing like that, you just have to escort someone to Japan. They're travelling on a fake passport but you go on your own and sit next to them on the plane, fill in their immigration forms or whatever, maybe you both dress up like businessmen, it's just so they feel comfortable going through customs at the other end, you get a free flight to Japan and a thousand bucks US, it's easy, one of my buddies from the army has done it a couple of times.

Aye, it doesn't sound too bad, I says, I'll think about it. Japan, I was thinking, sure that'd be all right something different for a change.

Obviously we'll tread carefully and check it out, Olly says, but this Mr Carson is into all sorts of stuff apparently so we'll get something.

Mr Carson, I goes, he's not Thai then.

I think he's from Singapore, Olly says, breathing a sigh of relief as the ferry pulls out, but who knows with these cunts.

They had a wee coffee machine on the ferry, sure I hadn't had coffee in ages, it was good so it was. The ferry wasn't that busy and it took two hours getting to the mainland so Olly stretched out across a couple of seats for forty winks. I wasn't tired, the coffee was making my head ping like a line of whizz, sure that's all speed is anyway. I walked out onto the deck for a look and spotted this gorgeous-looking wee blonde standing by herself looking nervous. She glanced over at me I could see she had a well-thumbed Lonely Planet under her arm so I walks over to say hello sort of thing.

Bout ye, I says, you tried this coffee it's not too bad actually.

Yes, she goes, I already had a cup it's quite strong isn't it.

You all right, I says, she looked like she'd been crying or something.

Yes, she goes, I'm just a bit worried about this town

Satun, there's nothing about it in the guidebook.

Is there not, I says, sure there's probably nothing worth seeing there that's all, I came through on the way down it's a bit of a shithole.

She bit her lip then and I realised I'd just made her even more nervous than she was before.

But don't worry about it, I says, me and my friend are staying there tonight so stick with us and you'll be all right.

She looked relieved then but I could tell she was a bit wary of me the way she was looking at my tatts and that. Loads of these backpackers think they're adventurous types until they come to some place not in their aul guidebook and then they're lost sure they depend on that aul thing far too much if you ask me.

I'm Billy, I goes and offers her my hand, and my mate Olly is sleeping through there, he's French but don't hold it against him if he tries to chat you up that's just his way.

She laughs a bit then and says, that's all right I'm used to it.

I'm sure you are, I goes, thinking I wouldn't mind this wee looker for myself and thank fuck Olly was dozing so's I could get in first.

I'm Sigrid, she says, from Stockholm. I'm meeting friends on Ko Samui.

Is that right, I goes, sure that'll be great craic it's dead nice over there so it is.

Oh good, she says relieved, is it easy to get there?

Aye, I says, just jump on one of the air-conditioned

buses in Satun they'll take you right up the coast sure I'll show you the morrow no problem.

Thanks so much, she goes, I feel better now I was a bit worried about sorting that out.

Tell me something, I goes, 'cos I always wondered this, is there no ugly people in the Sweden? I always thought the gorgeous blonde people were a myth but every one of youse that I meet looks like a supermodel or something, what do youse eat over there?

I could tell she liked hearing that 'cos she brushed her hair back over her ears then and smiled a bit. She was a right wee pocket rocket, absolutely gorgeous, perfect skin and lovely piercing blue eyes, in the back of my mind I was thinking I wouldn't mind retiring to the Sweden if they all look like this one, unbelievable so it was, quite a relief from that English bint with the hairy toes.

And every Irish guy I meet is a charmer, she goes, so I guess we both live up to the stereotype.

C'est vrai, I says, showing off.

Ah, tu parles français, she goes, I knew what she said but held my hands up, just a few words, I says, I suppose you speak twelve languages like everyone else from your part of the world.

Only five, she goes, like it was nothing.

Youse must have cracker schools like, I says.

She just shrugs, if you live in Europe you have to learn languages that's just the way it is.

Fuck me, I was thinking, sure I hardly understand nothing in my own language never mind no one else's,

I wish I'd paid attention in school then I thought our school was shite anyway even if I had listened, sure all they ever went on about was x plus y equals the sum of the square root and useless fucking bollocks like that, how was that going to prepare me for having a conversation with some wee honey from Sweden? No wonder the world thinks the Irish are a bunch of dumb Paddies only good for laying bricks and pushing wheelbarrows, sure the truth hurts we're fucking dopey cunts next to some of these Europeans.

We went inside and sat down for a bit. She was still nervous, I couldn't blame her looking at our sweaty gobs, but I calmed her down by going through her aul Lonely Planet and pointing out places I'd been and whether or not the guidebook was on the money or spouting a load of aul shite. When she asked me why I'd been on the road so long I told her the aul story about coming into some money after my parents were killed by the IRA and going off round the world to find myself. It was a load of bollocks of course and the first few times I said it to someone I nearly laughed when I got to the bit about finding myself but I was used to it by now and I knew it appealed to the women, look maybe it wasn't that far from the truth after all I had loads of friends shot or blown into wee sticky pieces by those Provo cunts and I was learning more with every person I met in the Thailand so in for a penny like, sure the more you say something sometimes the truer it becomes.

Sigrid was dead smart, she was in the third year of

some university course, environmental technology or something about how the planet was fucked up by us humans. She talked about it for a bit though I was lost most of the time until she started in about all the rubbish people dumped in the sea and that.

I've seen them do it, I says, it's disgusting so it is, I don't like that. I told her about this one time me and a couple of others went out in a boat to an island up north and the Thais bundled all our rubbish up into a plastic bag, the bottles and food wrappers and that, and turfed it over the side into the drink. I went mad so I did and told the cunt at the tiller to turn the boat around and pick it up. He just laughed and goes, what's the big deal. Some fish will eat that and die, I says. So what, he goes. So what? I says, so don't you cunts rely on fish for your dinner, what are you going to eat if the sea's full of plastic?

That's a huge problem, Sigrid goes.

Aye, I says, I couldn't believe it here we are in paradise and they're throwing aul bags into the water and spoiling it obviously I was leaving out all the cunts when I was speaking to her 'cos I didn't want to put her off of me. So next thing I slapped the Thai lad round the lugs, I says to her, lugs what's that she goes and I says, ears, right ha ha that's a funny word, anyway I says, he turned the boat round and went back and I took my shirt off and jumped in I thought he was going to drive off and leave me for a second but he was too feared. I grabbed the plastic bag and threw it back in the boat then climbed back in and says to him, don't do that again, what's wrong with you? He didn't get it and I suppose he probably just threw the bag in the sea later on when I wasn't looking but at least I tried, I says, sure it breaks your heart how they treat the place.

Good for you, she goes, if everyone did that maybe they'd think twice, the Irish are not big polluters like some of the other countries.

I don't know about that, I says to her, you walk down the Shankill Road where I'm from and there's all these chip wrappers whirling round in wee mini-tornadoes on the street corners, I'd skite any wee lad I saw throwing them down but what can you do people don't listen unless it affects them.

It's going to affect everybody that's the problem, she goes, shaking her head and looking severe.

Well good on ye for taking an interest, I says, we need a few more like you I reckon. She smiled all modest then and I was thinking fuck me if the world was full of women like this no cunt would ever get any work done sure you'd just be happy as Larry licking her clacker all day.

I was quite surprised when Olly woke up 'cos he wasn't that interested in her, sure I thought he'd be all over her but maybe she was a bit too classy for him or something. I think he was used to hanging around with a different type of women, ones he could take advantage of. I was pleased so I was 'cos if we liked different types then that was good there'd be no aul conflict, sure there's nothing worse than two lads fighting over some wee girl's hole, how pathetic is that like. Course you had to watch him I reckoned once your back was turned, he'd be in there like a flash and I didn't want him to say something stupid or disgusting that would wreck my wee Swedish fantasy.

Anyway the ferry docks at the mainland and we find ourselves with no way of getting into town, there was no taxis or tuk-tuks or nothing. All the other passengers on the ferry were locals, I suppose they weren't expecting three westerners at that time of the morning. Olly looks at me and says, how far is it to Satun can we walk, no way, I says, it's fucking miles away so it is and what about Sigrid, he gives her a dirty look like she's already some inconvenience and I says, haul on a minute there's some local lads with mopeds over there, I'll sort this out.

I goes over to these three hard-looking lads sitting on their bikes staring at us over their mirrored sunglasses and I says, bout ye lads, any chance of a lift into town sure we'll pay you for your trouble. One of them spoke a bit of English so him and me argued over the price for a bit, it does my head in but the Thais love it. I noticed that in the markets if you're buying an aul T-shirt or something the worst thing you can do is say how much is this like 'cos that lets them set the upper price and the cunts will say something outrageous like eight hundred baht and then you say I'll give you four hundred and by the end of the piece you're paying six hundred baht for some piece-of-shit T-shirt that you could of got for two hundred if you'd started the bidding in the first place by looking disgusted and saying here I'll give you fifty baht for this aul thing. They're sly but you can't blame them for taking advantage of the dumb-cunt westerners who're just here to fuck their daughters and wreck the place.

The lads agreed so we jumps on the back of the bikes, Sigrid was a bit nervous understandable like, but I says, don't worry we'll be all right if there's any trouble Olly and me we're well equipped to knock the fuck out of them, it wouldn't of surprised me if Olly had a piece on him and all. She needn't have worried, the lads knew their business and the ride into town was quite nice zooming through the countryside. The one I was holding onto turns to me as we're going along and says, you want happy-happy tonight, don't worry about me, I says to him, I'll sort myself out thanks very much.

He just ignores me and says, you want young girl I can get for you, what do you mean, I goes, not liking the sound of this, how young?

Ten, twelve years old he says, I get for you tonight you make happy-happy.

Get to fuck, I says to him, that's disgusting I'm not into that, you like older girls, he goes, I get you sixteen, seventeen.

Persistent fucker aren't ye, I says, maybe you didn't hear me I said no you dirty bastard, you're a bad man, I goes.

He just shrugs and laughs, men come over from Malaysia looking for young girl, he says, I give them business.

I was raging so I was if he hadn't of been driving the motorbike I'd of smacked him round the lugs it made me sad so it did thinking that every time he saw a white face like mine the first thing he thought was this fella's a kiddie fiddler, sure I'd only been in the country ten fucking minutes something needs to be done about the Thailand where evil fuckers like that can have their way with a wean.

Something similar must of happened with Olly 'cos when we gets into town and the lads take us direct to some dive of a guest house they were obviously getting a commission from, Olly jumps off and says, we're not staying here c'mon you two, what's going on, Sigrid says, grab your bag, I told her, trust me you don't want to be staying in this place we'll find somewhere better down the road. The three lads were raging that we didn't want to stay there but what could they do, Olly was striding away down the street I caught up to him with Sigrid trailing behind and says did they offer you a wee girl too, *Oui*, he goes, spitting in the gutter, *putain de cochons*.

What's that mean, I goes, knowing it wasn't good, fucking pigs, he says, *c'est vrai*, I goes, and he laughs, I'll have to teach you some more phrases.

Aye sounds good, I goes, I like the words, where we going anyway do you know?

Nah, he says, but there must be an old hotel or something round here that the backpackers don't know about. I want to meet some locals I hate all that backpacker talk, *what countries have you done* and all that, aye, I says, does my head in too, what's with her then, he goes, nodding in Sigrid's direction.

She'll be away in the morning, I says, just helping her out, he raises one eyebrow then and goes, sure sure you'll be helping her out of her clothes later on I suppose.

Give me a break, I says, she's fucking gorgeous so she is, do you not think so?

Olly just makes a face and goes, if you like that type she's too European for me, too boring, I'm into exotic women now. Sigrid catches up to us then and says something to him in the French, he laughs a bit and answers her back then winks at me and says, though maybe I could make an exception in this case.

It didn't take us long to find this amazing old crumbling hotel, it was obvious no backpackers ever stayed there 'cos the room we got for the three of us was dirt cheap and fucking huge, the ceilings were dead high, the whole thing was bigger than most houses back home, it wasn't luxury or nothing, the place had a real rundown feel to it but I liked it. This is perfect, Olly goes. There were two beds, one double for me and him and a single for Sigrid, she was happy enough with that and didn't seem bothered sharing with us. I suppose safety in numbers when you're in a strange place is the way to go like.

Olly started on her about not relying on the Lonely Planet and how you could have a much better time doing your own thing and she goes, yeah I see what you mean, it's good making your own decisions for a change, where do you reckon we can find something to eat I'm starving. Leave it to the Frenchman, Olly says, come on let's go out for a look around.

It was good having a bit of company for a change. I enjoyed myself knocking around Satun even though it was no great shakes, Olly was on his best behaviour around Sigrid, he was a bit more respectful than I thought he'd be and I could see her relaxing around us, here she was in some pisshole town thousands of miles from home all by herself and yet with us two around there was no way anything was going to happen to her. Olly discovered a wee French bakery, unbelievable so it was, so we ate some aul croissants in this poky wee park and then found the bus station so Sigrid could get her ticket sorted out for the morrow.

We spent the afternoon sitting in a café drinking coffee while Sigrid wrote in her journal and Olly and me avoided talking about what we'd been doing lately, giving each other the sanitised version so to speak so's not to shock the Swede. We had dinner and a few Changs later on, it was all very civilised I wasn't used to that but it reminded me of how normal people live. Olly and Sigrid chatted in the French, I didn't know what they were on about but I listened anyway and tried to pick up some words I was learning loads, by the end of the night my head was buzzing so it was. I hadn't used my brain so much in ages, trying to keep the fucker switched off so I wouldn't think about back home and that.

We got a couple of beers and took them back to the room. I had no idea what was going to happen, we'd been up since early that morning and I was about ready to crash but I was thinking should I make a move on Sigrid, sure she was leaving the next day and I'd never see her again but it was a bit funny with Olly being in the room, unless he went out for a walk or something there was no privacy. Anyway once we get in there it was dead hot and the aul ceiling fan wasn't helping much. Olly flopped down on the bed and started searching through his bag for something to open the beers, whilst he was doing that Sigrid peels off her shorts and T-shirt and ties her hair up, does anyone need to use the bathroom I'm grabbing a shower guys, she goes.

Olly shakes his head without batting an eyelid at the sight of her standing there in her bra and knickers.

I'm all right, I goes, thinking fuck me would you look at that she had a fucking perfect body and she was all sweaty, I just wanted to throw her down right there. Off she goes into the bathroom anyway, I looks at Olly and he's yawning.

I might listen to some music, he goes, and produces a battered aul Walkman. He puts the headphones on and props a pillow behind his head. In a couple of minutes he was snoring and I had to take the beer out of his hand so it wouldn't spill on the bed. The best I could hope for was that he'd turn over and sleep through whatever hijinks Sigrid and I got up to, not that there was a guarantee of anything happening at all but I was certainly going to try.

She comes out of the bathroom five minutes later with a towel wrapped round her and her underwear scrunched up in her hand, good shower, I goes, thinking fucking hell nice line, it was okay, she says, you having one, aye good idea, I says, knowing that when a girl asks if you're taking a shower what she means is you should take a shower. I was in and out of there in a flash 'cos the water was cold but that done me good and I walked back out all nonchalant sort of thing with the towel wrapped round my waist.

Sigrid was sitting on the edge of her bed with the towel still on but she had one foot up and was running a wee nail file over her toes. I could see right up her towel and there it was, the holy grail, the sweetest little peach fanny lips I ever saw in my life and a wee tuft of creamy blonde hair above them. I don't think she had any idea she was exposing herself to me, it wasn't like she was doing it to get me going or anything she was so absorbed in what she was doing giving herself a pedicure or something, yon English bint could of taken a leaf out of her book.

I was stood there like some schoolboy waiting for permission and I started thinking fuck me what if she's not interested and I have to climb into bed next to Olly with my bollocks hanging in the wind how embarrassing. She finishes up what she's doing and puts her leg back down, thank fuck I was trying not to look. She cranes her neck to see what Olly's doing and says to me, is he asleep?

Aye, he's out for the count I goes, good, she says, and

reaches into her wee toiletries bag. She pulls out a strip of four flunkies and tears one off all casual like, setting it dead careful on the bed.

What's going on, I says, like a fucking eejit, come on, she goes, take your towel off and lie down here, well I wasn't going to say no was I, so I done what I was told sure I'd a raging stiff one by this stage. Sigrid takes her own towel off, fuck me what a sight I could hardly believe I was going to do it with such a honey, casual as fuck she rips open the flunky and rolls it down my aul knob like an expert, no foreplay straight down to it, I says, she just smiles all cryptic like and says, no that's too intimate, we don't know each other. I wanted to say and sticking my knob inside you's not intimate, love? but I knew to keep my mouth shut.

She fishes back inside her bag then and produces this wee tube of lube. She rubs it on my knob and then puts some on herself, it was a bit cold like but I could see where she was going with all this she just wanted a good aul slow screw, I could understand sometimes that's the best, no pissing around, anyway she straddles me and slides my knob inside her, she winced a bit 'cos she wasn't dead wet or nothing but after a wee minute it was all good, the aul lube was doing its job and she lowers herself completely down the length of me and does this big exhale sort of thing.

She just sat there with her eyes closed not moving for a bit but I didn't mind 'cos it was like having the fucking goddess Aphrodite sitting on your knob. I ran my hands dead gentle like up her sides and over her tits and stomach down to her pubes just stroking her, barely touching the skin, she put her arms up and pushed her fingers through her hair, biting her lip a wee bit, fuck me there's an image you'll not forget in a hurry Billy I was thinking, sure there's not a single woman looks anything like her in Northern Ireland, maybe if there was a few thousand of them there'd be no Troubles, sure you don't see the Swedes fighting the piece out or blowing each other up or nothing no wonder with honeys like this to keep them busy.

Anyway slow as you like she starts grinding on me, sliding up and down on my aul knob sure I was tensing it like fuck so's to keep it hard to please her, it was fucking beezer so it was, she was going dead slow and rubbing her tits and putting her hand between her legs and moving her head around throwing her hair back and stuff, she fucked like a world champion and there was me just lying there watching all right obviously she wasn't into me that much, she just wanted a stiff aul knob to bounce up and down on but I wasn't complaining. I sort of lost track of the time, I was just glad Olly was sleeping.

She had control of my knob better than I did myself, the aul traitor was obeying her every command. She took it to the edge and then stopped for just a second or two with her back arched and eyes rolling back in her head, fingers digging into my chest and then she powered home hair flying all over the place. It wasn't too bad for me either, I could hardly focus on her at all it felt like a fucking gallon of jizz flew out of me, the sensation went right up my spine into the base of my skull and all I could see was white light, it felt like the fucking sun had exploded inside my head.

I can't even 'member her climbing off of me, all I know is that she lay in the crook of my arm for a bit 'cos her hair was in my mouth and just as I could feel myself drifting away with these warm waves rolling up my chest she gave me this wee soft kiss on the lips and whispered, thank you, fuck sake if she'd said marry me or write me a cheque for a million dollars or will you turn Fenian for me I'd of said yes anything anything you want just don't move stay with me I hope this moment never ends, but instead I just fell asleep.

When I woke up the next morning she was gone. I was a bit cut up about it and Olly kept me going saying I was in love and shite like that, maybe I was, I didn't care anyway. Sure I'd be in love with whatever come along next too and maybe that would just be for a night as well. The Swedish would just be another memory, some fantasy from the past I could hardly 'member like I'd been living the life of some other fucker, a lucky one too, but someone that wasn't me. With all I'd done, with all the shite that was in my head, I didn't deserve any of this.

Olly wanted to travel on the local buses between towns and work our way slowly up to the Bangkok. I didn't mind actually, sure I caught one of them fancier coaches one time and near froze my bollocks off. They had the aircon pumping it was like a fucking meat locker or something in there, all the westerners like me were in shorts and T-shirts and the Thais had to hand out blankets to keep people warm, it was fucking stupid so it was, sure the sun was belting down outside, just turn it down fuck sake I says but they wouldn't. I couldn't see the sense in it for the life of me.

The local buses were better as they took their time and went down the back roads so at least you got to see a bit of the aul countryside. Plus there was no backpackers on them only locals that were all curious about us, they didn't understand why we weren't on the coaches. We tried explaining to them that this way was loads cheaper and more interesting but they just didn't get it, sure they think all westerners are loaded with money, one aul cunt asked Olly what sort of car did he drive in his country a BMW or Mercedes, he just laughed and goes, a bicycle what do you take me for, the aul bastard nearly died he couldn't believe we didn't have Ferraris and speedboats and villas on the Côte d' fucking Azur.

I actually do have a vintage Mercedes in storage, Olly goes to me later, not that I'll ever see it again.

Aye I says, whispering to him, my boss gave me his 5 Series Beemer when he got a new one but I had to torch the cunt, fucking blood all over the back seat, even Mr Muscle couldn't get that out.

Some of the towns we stopped at were pure shite and there was nothing worth seeing or doing at all, no wonder they weren't in the aul Lonely Planet but others were all right, at least they had a night market where you could get some good scran though finding skirt to satisfy Olly's yellow fever was a bit harder so to speak. I don't know why they call it yellow fever actually, I never met no one from anywhere in Asia who looked yellow to me sure I had darker skin than most of them, it's just fucking aul racist talk I suppose, probably the English started it. Anyway the bus journeys were always a laugh, Olly would go and sit next to some Thai woman and try to chat her up, he must of done some of their heads in. I'd just sit and read my book and mind my own business whilst he got slapped in the mouth for sliding his hand up some girl's skirt at the back of the bus.

The best was when these two aul ladies got on, sure we knew straightaway they'd been on the game you could just tell but they were well past retirement age now. They spotted us and came over to sit down they spoke English pretty good and they were a laugh, they wanted to practise their phrases probably so's they could do a bit of business sort of thing. The one that was sitting beside me produces an aul phrasebook, it was ancient so it was, it didn't even call the country Thailand it said Siam which was what the place was called until Hitler come along. It was like from the forties or something written for the western gentleman, fucking hilarious so it was, she gave it to me and then fell asleep on my shoulder like I was her fucking husband or something.

I flicked through and near pished myself laughing at the phrases they thought a man about town might need back then. It wasn't like one of them French phrasebooks they have in schools, *où est la piscine* and all that shite, this was getting down to business. *I would like to enjoy myself with a woman, can you get one for me?* it says, aye right enough I was thinking, at least they're honest. *When will the Third World War break out?* Fuck sake, sure when this was written the second one was still on and here they are worrying about the third and besides what would some Thai fella in the street know about that? How're you supposed to answer that in 1943? Not for another couple of years probably pal don't worry about it, anyway do you want to go and see a woman fire ping-pong balls out her snatch, you do, right just down here mate.

There was all this shite about gloves too. *I can guarantee the durability of these gloves* what the fuck's that all about, were gloves a major export industry back then? *Douglas Fairbanks acts very well indeed* was another one. Jesus sure that shows how old it was, wasn't he Tarzan or Robin Hood or something? The best was this wee exchange which I memorised in the Thai 'cos it sounded dead handy.

I want a woman.
Yes, I shall find one for you. Do you like this one?
Yes, I like her very much. Call me a tricycle.

Fucking pisser that is, like. Imagine going up to some cunt in the street and saying I want a woman just like that and then wouldn't you know he just happens to have one handy and she fits the bill, probably his daughter or his wife or something. Fucking disgusting this place I was thinking, sure they'll sell you anything that's not nailed down even the phrasebooks in the forties had sample conversations with pimps but the best part has got to be the bit about the tricycle, sure is that what they had for taxis back then, did yer man and his whore have to stand on the back whilst some wee Thai fucker pedalled like fuck to the nearest hotel, pure madness so it is, fucking economy based on glove-making and prostitution though they seemed to have done away with the gloves these days.

So we come to this wee town called Chumphon, don't know where they got the names of these places from though I suppose they could say the same about our towns, Ballymena Armagh Glengormley or whatever, the only reason they don't sound fucking stupid is 'cos you grow up saying them, for all I know Antrim means knob jockey or something in the Thai.

Anyway we jumped off the aul bus in Chumphon and checked into this wee guesthouse down a back street though it seemed to be all back streets. The Thai girl on reception spoke dead good English, the best I'd heard. Olly tried to chat her up but she gave him such a dirty look he let it go sharpish. I felt sorry for her, I was thinking every western cunt that came into the place must of tried it on with her, what a pain in the arse. Anyway Olly heads on up to the room for a shower muttering under his breath and I hung back to say sorry to the wee girl.

Don't pay him no mind, I says, sure he's French.

So? she goes, is that an excuse for being a letcher?

Steady on love, I says, it goes both ways you know, sure I've been offered all sorts of services by the locals, I feel like a fucking walking dollar sign sometimes not to mention an aul perve, we're not all sex tourists you know, it does my head in too.

She gave me a good looking-over then and let out a big sigh. Well sorry about that, she says, please excuse me for being so rude I shouldn't jump to conclusions, she sounded a bit sarcastic but I waved it off, don't worry about it, I goes, sure how long you been working here no offence but you sound dead educated or something.

Thanks for noticing, she goes, you're right of course I shouldn't be here at all but jobs in the tourist industry are about all a woman can get. I'm actually a chartered accountant.

You're kidding me on, I says, sure what the fuck you doing behind the desk there excuse my language miss.

What. The fuck. Am I. Doing. Here. She said it all spaced out like that and straightaway I knew I'd be pals with her, sure I felt exactly the same way even though I was on the other side of the desk every desk has two sides to it doesn't it though and sometimes one's just as bad as the other.

Is there no jobs in the accountancy then, I says, well I do a bit here, she goes, but getting into one of the big firms is basically impossible if you're a woman.

What about in other countries, I says, sure your English is better than mine could you not go to the Australia or somewhere like that.

All very well saying that, she goes, but having the money to go is out of the question, I'll have to work here for about five years just to save enough, never mind what you have to do to get a visa.

That's proper fucked, I says, sure what sort of world have we created like.

Tell me about it, she goes. Anyway what's your story, she looks down at the guest register and goes, Billy Montgomery, you don't look much like the average fisherman-pant-wearing tourist. You look more like you just got out of prison.

Not a bad guess, I goes, but I was thinking fuck me is it that obvious maybe I should try blending in a bit more, anyway she had my number right enough so I figured there was no sense lying to her. Aye look, I says, I been in your country more than a year now sure I can't go back home 'cos I got into a wee spot of trouble over there. I've got money and that so I'm all right but still it's a funny aul life just wandering from place to place with no rhyme or reason, you know what I mean.

I've seen men like you before, she goes, usually former soldiers looking to lose themselves for a while and forget who they were. Is that what's happening with you?

It was a bit close to the bone, and when she said the words I knew that about summed it up. I suppose I was a kind of soldier even though there were some who would have said freedom fighter and others who would have said terrorist or paramilitary, I never really thought about it in them terms in fact I didn't like thinking about it at all. Ever since Big Jim sent me over to the Thailand I'd had way too much time to think about what I'd done, never mind how good the beaches and the honeys were. Sure how many 23-year-olds would have fucked people up the way I done, fucking drill bits to kneecaps and baseball bats to elbows and bits of brain oozing out the back of skulls, it's bound to affect ye in the end sure all I was doing was waiting for it to hit me and the only reason it hadn't bothered me so far was that I was so desensitised to it from being a Loyalist from a young age. I'd probably need all my money just to pay for the therapy or whatever though fuck knows maybe prison or a Provo's bullet to the head would've been better for me, sometimes I reckon the worst thing that can happen to a person is surviving.

Something like that, I says to her, it doesn't bear thinking about really. I don't know why I was being so honest with her, I didn't even know her or nothing but it's always the strangers you confide in, sure for someone like me there's nobody else. Even with our Olly I had to watch myself, he knew plenty enough already.

Look I get off in half an hour, she goes, if you can lose your friend I'll walk you to the night market for something to eat and make sure you don't get ripped off or end up eating the arse end of a rat. I laughed, is that what them wee things were sure I didn't mind them, I suppose they're an acquired taste. You're on, I says, I'll meet you back down here in thirty. I feel bad now, I don't even know your name. It's Quan, she goes, a nice easy one.

Back in the room Olly was getting dressed in the aul sweaty clothes he'd just taken off but he'd cheered up a bit. Did you find out where the brothels are from that bitch downstairs, he goes.

Shut your gob, I says, do you not think about nothing else?

Look at the big man in love again, he goes. I didn't know you were so soft, Billy.

Away and fuck, I says, I think we need a wee break from each other before I burst ye.

He leaned back on the bed then with his arms behind his head looking me up and down. You just let me know the time and place *mon ami*, he goes, you may be used to everyone shitting themselves when you get angry but I think you'll find me a different proposition.

I was about ready to jump the cunt right there and then. I wasn't scared of him or nothing but I knew if we came to blows we'd fucking wreck the place, it would be one of those big fights that lasts twenty minutes and we'd probably half kill each other, we'd both be down the nearest hospital for sure with broken bones and punctured lungs and what have ye.

Aye sure let me consult my diary, I says, and I'll slot ye in, it'd be my pleasure.

He laughs then and gets up to put his aul manky boots on. *Bon*, he goes, I'm going out to look for some action, are you coming with me or having a candlelit dinner with your new girlfriend?

I just gave him a look and he raised his hands. *T'inquiéte pas*, he goes, *je me casse*.

Aye, I says, *cassez-vous, conard*.

He smiled then and says, no no you only use *vous* in a formal setting or if you're addressing a stranger or using the plural. Because we're friends you have to *tutoyer*.

Oh right that's a bit complicated, I says, what do I say then, *casse-toi*?

Yes! he goes, that's good, now you're getting it.

So anyway right Olly fucked off to look for his own entertainment and I went back downstairs to meet Quan and we wandered up to the night market in the main square. I always liked them places, it was like every cunt in the town all descended upon the same spot to have a bite to eat and an aul yarn. Everyone seemed to know everyone else, it was one of them sense-of-community sort of deals. I wasn't used to it sure the closest thing we had back home was when we all lined up to throw bricks at Fenian kids on their way to school through our estate, at least that was a bloody good laugh.

The aul scran smelt gorgeous so it did, the only problem was I didn't know what the fuck half of it was and most of the Thais serving it didn't speak much English if any at all. I learned pretty quick that if you said is this chicken they'd just nod and say yes! chicken! even if what you were pointing at had half a dozen tentacles. Having Quan with me made all the difference like. Not only did she know what everything was but she made sure we only paid the local prices, sure they add loads on for the *farangs*, that's Thai for foreigners.

It was dead good, so it was, sitting there in the warm surrounded by loads of families and that, wee kids running about playing and dogs fighting with each other happy as you like. Most of the aul places you go in Thailand are all set up to cater for the tourists so you never get to see how the real people live, even though Olly was a pain in the arse at least his idea of working our way to Bangkok by local buses was sound, you felt like you were really seeing the country rather than the aul postcard version they spoon feed ye.

Problem was, poor aul Quan started to get funny looks from some of the locals. These three cunts went past on their mopeds and said something to her, I didn't understand it obviously but I could tell from the tone it wasn't complimentary. Some of the stallholders were giving her scolding looks too.

What's the deal, I goes, what'd them fuckers say to ye? I'll burst them if they insulted ye or something.

She scowled, not at me but at whatever was going on. I should have known better, she goes, I didn't think.

What is it, tell me, I says.

Because I'm seen with you here people will think I'm a prostitute now.

I was fucking raging so I was. What do you mean, I says, sure don't they all know ye, what would they think that for?

It's stupid I know, she goes, but the way they look at it there's no other reason for a Thai girl to be seen with a *farang*.

Catch yourself on, I says, that's a load of aul bollocks. Sure we're just friends having a wee bite to eat, there's nothing funny about it. Is it not possible for you to be pals with a westerner without sex coming into the equation?

I know it is, she goes, but this is Thailand. She looks around dead nervous then, the lads on the mopeds were lurking down the road and revving their stupid wee engines. If you're finished we should go, she says, I do not want to have a problem later. My reputation, you understand.

Fuck me I was mortified. I jumped up straightaway, aye aye of course like c'mon let's go I'm really sorry, Quan. I never thought of that.

We took the quiet streets to get back to the guest-house, that was her idea I wasn't keen in case them cunts on the mopeds tried to start something but I was so raging I'd of knocked the fuck out of the lot of them even if they were tooled up. No one bothered us though and we just walked back pretty much in silence. I could see Quan was thinking about all the explaining she was going to have to do and how she probably wouldn't even be able to convince loads of people 'cos you know what people are like the world over, fucking aul gossips so they are, nothing better to do with their time.

I could hardly talk anyway for the sick feeling in the pit of my stomach. I hardly felt so wretched in my life, well most of it anyhow, even with all the bad stuff I done back home, sure that was par for the course in Belfast but over here I didn't like the idea of ruining some wee girl's reputation over nothing, that fucked me up so it did. I'd fucked around with a couple of wee whores just for the novelty of it but now I felt like a right dirty bastard. The aul sex tourism had changed things for all these people, I could see that now 'cos normal life no longer existed. It was kind of like how the Troubles had changed things back home, once you go down that road sure there's no going back, everything gets changed forever and not for the better. I felt ashamed so I did.

Back at the guesthouse Quan apologised to me for how the evening had turned out, fucking nearly broke my heart so it did, don't you apologise, I goes, I'm the one who should be saying sorry to you and your people for all we've done to ye.

Don't worry, she says, patting my hand, it's good that at least you know all Thai women are not for sale. Off she went to her room then and left me standing in the foyer, an aul creeping familiar feeling of having fucked something up twisting a knot in my gut. Two dogs barked at each other somewhere in the distance and it started to rain. Sure if it wasn't for the heat and mosquitoes buzzing around my neck I might as well of been back home.

Stopping at all these wee out of the way places was all very well. We were avoiding the backpackers and all the aul tourist shite, brilliant, what a couple of aul martyrs seeing the real country and all that, the only problem being it was a pain in the arse sometimes so it was. Sure we would turn up in places like Prachuap Khiri Khan that obviously hadn't seen any palefaces like us in fucking ages which meant all the locals would be staring at us and pointing and giggling and whatnot, it does your head in after a while and then there's the whole drama of getting a place to stay when the town's obviously not set up for tourists and no cunt speaks a word of English. No offence to them like, I don't expect them to speak the lingo of some country thousands of miles away that they're never going to visit, it's just that after a while I realised that all this avoiding doing the same thing as the other *farangs* was just making life difficult for me and the Frenchy.

It's not like we were getting on great or nothing. He was wanting to dip his wick into as many local girls as possible whereas I'd lost the appetite for that sort of thing with just about anyone. We'd shacked up in this shithole of a place in Prachuap which was basically a town with a couple of aul beaches on that dead thin strip of land right in the middle of Thailand not far from Burma really, though why any fucker would want to go there is beyond me. I was getting impatient with all this stopping and starting and I was thinking the best thing to do would just be to scoot right on up to the Bangkok where at least there'd be civilisation of some sort. I needed some company that wasn't French for a change though I was learning loads of good words, I wasn't bad at picking up the aul languages. I think maybe I missed my calling as a translator at the United Nations for yon fella Boutros Boutros-Ghali.

The room we had at the guesthouse was basically a big fucking cupboard and there was only one bed with an aul manky mattress, the locals must of thought we were arse bandits or something not that it would've bothered them 'cos when we went for a walk down the main street there was loads of trannies doing the rounds and cooing at us. Olly thought it was dead funny until I pointed out that the only fannies he'd be looking up round here would probably be knobs sliced down the middle and turned inside out. He didn't like the sound of that but all the same he took some wee slip of a thing that was hanging around the guesthouse out for a drink somewheres. I mean she looked like a woman to me, she'd no big Adam's apple protruding or broad shoulders or chiselled jaw line like yer man Judge Dredd in the comics, but sure you've no way of telling till you've got a mouthful of ball sack and if you get that far sure you might as well go the whole hog and admit you're not bothered.

Anyway he was off on his hot date and after wandering round the docks for a bit getting wolf whistles from tons of ladyboys I headed on back to the room to read my book, sure Olly had got me a copy of this wee book called *The Outsider* by some French cunt, he said it was brilliant. I wasn't sure at first but it didn't take me long getting into it, yer man Camus knew what he was on about, sure it was like he knew what I was thinking. My life wandering about with no fucking purpose not even thinking about what I was doing or where I was going next was just like in some of them books, Kerouac and them ones, that's what made me think maybe I should write it all down one day if I was banged up in the Maze or the Bangkok Hilton or somewhere, it might not be written as nice or nothing 'cos I'm no good with words but you never know some cunt might want to read it if they're bored as fuck on an aul long bus trip or something.

There was no sink or bog in the room, not even an aul squat toilet but then we were on the first floor so it's a bit of a long drop for your shite I suppose, anyway I wandered downstairs to wash my face in the sink and I left the door to the room open. I wasn't worried 'cos I could see the bottom of the stairs from the toilet, I'm dead paranoid but for good fucking reason. Sure enough it only took ten seconds for this cunt to appear out of nowhere and run up the stairs, he must of been watching me and thought I went out for a bit or was taking a dump. He took the stairs three at a time and hardly made a sound, just as well I seen him from where I was standing just inside the bathroom otherwise I would of been clueless, he was like a fucking ninja or something.

I waited for about ten seconds to give him plenty of time to get into the room and then quiet as you like I padded up the stairs after him. I had my shirt off 'cos I was sweating, in fact all I was wearing was a pair of aul Y-fronts that'd seen better days but I was about three times his size. Butterflies started up in my guts at the thought of bursting someone especially an aul thief, sure there's nothing worse.

When I got to the door of the room I could see him inside with his back to me and he was going through this aul leather bumbag that Olly usually carried on him, it had his passport and his bank cards and a load of money in there, the thief must of thought this was his lucky day. He was so absorbed in what he was doing he didn't hear me coming up behind him.

I just stood there leaning on the door jamb casual as you like with my arms crossed watching him, there was no way he was getting past me and no other way out of the room unless he smashed the window and jumped out into the alleyway but it was a bit of a drop like. He thought about taking stuff out of Olly's bumbag and then decided against it and just threw the whole thing over his shoulder, smart move, that's what I would of done if I was a piece-of-shit dumb cunt too. He started eyeing off my backpack and took a step towards it, greedy cunt I thought, you deserve everything I'm going to give to ye.

Bout ye, I says, I'm from pest control. I hear there's a wee vermin problem. The cunt near jumped out of his skin. He threw Olly's bumbag down on the floor and took one step toward me then thought the better of it and stepped back, he was looking all round the room for a way out but he must of known he was trapped. I just stood there waiting for him to work it out. No trouble no trouble, he says, I just checking room make sure you okay, he was agitated as fuck as you would be like seeing a big cunt like me standing over ye and knowing you were going to get a right aul hiding.

I like a bit of verbal sparring before getting stuck into someone just to see what they come up with. I wasn't expecting much from this one but I thought I'd give him a chance all the same, sure I felt a wee tiny bit sorry for him, not much like but you know it's a dangerous profession he'd chosen.

So explain to me what you're doing exactly, I goes, you could see his mind racing at the thought he might just be able to talk his way out of the situation if only he could find the right words.

I work for hotel, he says, not stealing come to check see if you okay when I see door open I think you forget and better take valuables put in safe to stop thief very bad, you be more careful sir lot of thief here.

Not bad, I was thinking. That's very kind of you looking after your guests like that, I goes, I've never seen such excellent service, what's your name pal I'm going to say something to the manager and recommend you get a pay rise. He was a bit confused by this, it was kinda cruel really, sure I was just toying with him. Not necessary sir, he says, part of service happy to help I love *farang*, where you from England very great country Manchester United Eric Cantona.

I put my fingers up to my lips and made like to zip them closed, he shut the fuck up then. You were doing all right there, I says to him, until you got to the bit at the end, sure I fucking hate Man United that's a Fenian team and I'm a Liverpool man, you just insulted me big time. I was just rolling the muscles in my neck ready for a bursting when I hear Olly coming up the stairs behind me muttering to himself.

Just in time, I goes, sure we've got a guest, how'd your date go, did she have a big knob? Olly looks at me confused then he sees yer man quaking in his boots next to the bed.

I didn't know you went both ways, he goes, do you want me to give you two lovebirds fifteen minutes?

I laughed then and pointed to Olly's bumbag lying on

the ground. He put two and two together pretty quick, you have to hand it to him he was sharp as a tack our Olly.

Oh I see, he says, nice as you like with a big smile, that sort of guest, well don't be so rude Billy close the door and let's make him welcome. The whole time he was cracking his knuckles, the Thai fella pissed himself when I shut the door. I knew 'cos it was that familiar aul smell of fear, it took me right back so it did.

Olly wasn't too keen on splashing out on one of them luxury air-conditioned coaches but I insisted like, even if we were going to freeze our nuts off. Sure I was sick of the aul local buses, they were dead hot and if you didn't have any food on ye you were fucked, they'd pick these scrawny fuckers up by the side of the road and they'd walk down the bus with a big stick over their shoulder with all these wee plastic bags hanging off of it. I don't know what was inside, sure it looked like sick or something, loads of wee bits floating around in there but they were selling it anyway and the locals always snapped it up and sucked it down with an aul straw. Near turned my stomach so it did but sure if you're starving you'll eat anything. I was worried about getting a dose of the runs, it's not like there's service stations with lovely pristine toilets every ten miles it's more a case of squirting out your lunch in a festy ditch with all the people on the bus watching ye. Best avoided really.

Under duress the Frenchman agreed to take a flash coach up to the Bangkok, it was good so it was, sure they had TV screens and everything and they showed a film *The Nutty Professor* with yer man Eddie Murphy in a fatsuit. I overheard one of the backpackers on the bus saying fuck me that hasn't even come out yet in Europe, I suppose the Thais had a pirate tape of it or something, that seems to be their way. It was a load of aul shite but my eyes were glued to the screen sure I hadn't seen a film in about six months, it's funny how quick you forget about the so-called civilised world when you're hiding out on some wee island doing nothing but shagging backpackers and eating green chicken curry and getting hammered on Chang.

There was a couple of all-right-looking western girls on the bus, I heard a Scottish accent and even an American one, sure you don't see many of them ones they mustn't travel or something. Olly wasn't interested of course, too much trouble for him having to act like he gave a fuck. I wasn't fussed either to be honest, I was too busy getting my jollies with all the wee comforts like a flush toilet and a seat that didn't smell like someone's armpit.

Olly had run out of batteries for his Walkman and sure mine had gone the way of the dodo after the ants got to it. I'd have to buy me a new one in the Bangkok or maybe splash out on a CD one except I'd no CDs but that would be easy remedied by a trip to the Khao San Road, sure you could buy anything you wanted there and even some stuff you didn't realise you wanted yet. There was nothing else for it but for me and the Frenchman to have a yarn.

Do ye 'member, I says, yon time your pals in Algeria who got us those guns wanted six cars as payment instead of cash that was weird wasn't it, whatever happened to them?

Olly grinned then and sat up straight, Yusuf and his crew, yeah I remember we had some good times down in Marseille me and him but fuck he was mad you know he had eight sisters in Chlef not a pretty one amongst them and he was always trying to find them husbands, fucking hell he offered me twenty kilos of hash just to take one off his hands.

Pimping his sisters out that's charming that is, we could never work out what he wanted the cars for with all the money they had could they not just buy their own cars, they wanted dead specific makes too not even that good.

They were for his sisters, I think. He didn't want them to have BMWs that would draw too much attention.

Right, I says, that makes sense but still what did he want cars from us for unless maybe they'd be harder to trace or something.

Yeah maybe, Olly goes, I don't know, I didn't ask too many questions, I'll tell you what though they were a bitch to get over there without arousing suspicion, I had to rent a shipping container and bribe about a dozen customs officials it cost me a fortune and I had to use up a couple of favours, it was easier getting the guns to you boys.

Aye well I suppose nobody says boo if they see an army truck driving around with a bunch of Armalites in the back but half a dozen Ford Fiestas are a bit harder to disguise like. Is Yusuf and them ones still in business?

Well he got shot in the leg and the last time I saw him he was on crutches but I didn't use him after that, the fucking cops were all over him for the turf war in Marseille, it was a bad scene and I didn't want it to lead back to me. He's either dead or in jail now I suppose.

Aye most of our ones are as well. Same for me too if I hadn't come out here.

Olly just nods. I've been meaning to ask you, he says, why are you out here anyway, I mean with me it's just a case of avoiding debts basically and saving my own skin it's not like I'm on the ten-most-wanted list but you and your crew up there well don't tell me anything I can't deny in court later but you had a civil war going on, correct me if I'm wrong.

Aye, I laughs, thinking it's not very funny what the fuck are you laughing for, that's just a front though, I says.

Oh come on, he goes, you're just saying that because I'm Catholic, tell the truth, Billy, everyone knows it's a religious war between your boys and ours it's all over the news.

Oh aye? I says. You tell me what it's about then.

He was a bit defensive then, like I'd offended him or something.

Well, he goes, all slow and careful, as far as I know the Catholic minority want a united Ireland so the IRA are fighting to get the English to leave but your side wants to stay part of the UK. That's about the size of it, *non*?

Nice and simple isn't it, I goes, and maybe that's how it was at the start a long fucking time ago but let me burst your bubble here by telling ye a wee story. Every fortnight me, my brother Mark and my boss Big Jim Gallagher would have a meet at a nice wee café down the city centre, cappuccino and a caramel slice sort of thing. You know who would join us? Three lads from the other side of the wall, this dead funny cunt called Liam, I loved him so I did he was great craic, Declan was another one, he was the muscle like me so he never said much, I always wondered if I could take him but never found out, and the third one was their boss man Shay, he was the brains fuck he was smart just like Big Jim sure the two of them got on like nobody's business. They'd both been to Queen's University when they were younger sure that's where they met.

Anyway we would all have an aul yarn about business just to make sure we weren't steppin' on each others toes sort of thing, we'd even help each other out sometimes or if there was a new shopping centre opening up someone would bring the plans along and we'd work out what we were going to do about it. If there was a lot of jobs tied up in the construction contracts then once the place was near finished we'd blow it up, our side or theirs it didn't matter sure we'd take turns, the important thing was that the place was reduced to rubble so all the lads working on it would have another year or two's employment. Everyone knew so they'd all make themselves scarce so no cunt got hurt unless we wanted rid of someone in which case we'd stick them in the back of the van loaded up with Semtex, kill two birds with one stone you know. Anyway there's only so many times you can blow a place up, apart from the Europa Hotel that is, sure we done that more than twenty times.

Didn't Clinton stay there last year, Olly says.

Aye sure it's lovely when it's in one piece. I stayed there myself a couple of times, good food. As I was saying eventually we had to let places like Castle Court get built but once they were it was a goldmine we'd meet Shay and the lads to divvy up the protection money, it was dead funny sometimes I 'member us arguing over who was going to shake down Toys 'R' Us. Shay and Liam had weans so they wanted it.

That was only the tip of the iceberg between us and them sure we ran gambling, drugs, prostitution and everything else you can think of not to mention taking our cut of government contracts for reconstruction and all that shite. There used to be this big mural on the Shankill estate, it said ALL DRUG DEALERS WILL BE SHOT like we were guardians of the community or something, what a joke, course you read between the lines and what it really says is all drug dealers who don't work for us will be shot. We're businessmen, that's all there is to it, no different from the Mafia or your drug lords. This aul peace process? We don't want that so we don't, that's bad for business.

Olly was nodding, he could see the sense in it, sure he done deals with all sorts of fuckers us included.

Still, he goes, a lot of people have got killed so you and the rest can make money does that not bother you.

Course it does, I says, there's not a day goes by I don't think about some of the poor cunts we done over especially now when I've got too much time on my hands, it's going to fuck me up so it is but what can you do sure we're not the first ones to go down this road.

Olly looked disgusted and sort of disappointed. I'd seen that look on people's faces before when I gave them the lowdown.

I know what you're thinking, I says, you thought there was something romantic about the struggle sure you're not the only one, there's thousands of Americans give money to the IRA every year thinking they're helping out freedom fighters or something, what a laugh the whole thing's one big fucking joke, the UDA the INLA the UVF the Provos and every bunch of lads with guns and Semtex it's in their interest to keep the Troubles going on forever, sure you know how ye can spot a terrorist in Belfast? He's the one wearing a tracksuit and a baseball cap, driving a BMW 7 Series.

Everyone knows who we are but they're all too scared

and I was thinking it might be about time for me to check into the Ritz for a week just so's I wouldn't go mental. Olly wouldn't hear talk of it mind sure he'd sleep in a ditch rather than pay money for a bed, he must of been running low on funds or something that was why he didn't mind us shooting on up to Bangkok so he could line up a wee job with yer man Mr Carson he'd talked about. It sounded like trouble but sure I'd a contact in Bangkok myself I intended looking up when Olly wasn't about, I'd a wee plan of my own brewing.

The Bangkok's wild so it is, sure there's loads to do, Buddhist temples and that to see if that's your thing. Just ask the driver of one of them tuk-tuks to take ye and he will right enough no bother, happy to help as long as you don't mind spending two and a half hours being fitted for an aul cheap suit by his brother-in-law's second cousin twice removed in a backstreet tailor's conveniently located about ten miles in the opposite direction. Or else you could take a wander down the Khao San market and buy yourself a lovely pad thai cooked in an upturned bin lid, might give ye the gastro but sure that's part of the experience.

The safest way to spend your afternoon is probably to go to one of the sex shows down in Patpong sure they've got everything the westerner wants to see pussy opens bottle, fish in pussy and yer aul favourite the classic ping-pong ball act, sure it never gets stale though how minging is it? I'm sure they don't sterilise those balls between acts and I don't know how often they change them, it's not like fucking Wimbledon.

Aye sure the whole place is fucked in the head, you get pestered constantly. I was thinking of carrying three Polaroids round in my pocket, one of me wearing a suit that was three times too big with the arm hanging off of it, one of me puking my guts up in a gutter somewhere and the third one of my knob after I'd given it a good aul going over with a wire brush. That way when I get stopped in the street for the five-thousandth time by some Thai cunt offering me one of their essential services I could show him the photos and say, already bought it ate it caught it, get away to fuck.

Olly was keen to make some money so he called yon Mr Carson fella and set up a meet. He had to contact him through some pissy wee travel agency, it must of been a front or something. I didn't like going in to those sorts of things without being tooled up but there wasn't time to sort something out, the best I could do was to buy an aul flick knife from some dodgy fucker down the market. What's that for, Olly says, making sandwiches, I goes, we'll not be needing that, he says, aye well better safe than sorry, I goes, sure I've no idea what you're getting us into here. We'll be all right, Olly says, I've had friends work for him before.

I clocked the Rolex on this Carson cunt as soon as he shook my hand. He was wearing a dead nice shirt open at the neck with cufflinks and everything and a wee gold necklace, he'd obviously had a haircut quite recent like sure he was well presented no doubt about it he looked the real deal though you can't tell in places like the Thailand where there's so much fake gear going around. We met him in this café in the south of the city, it took us a while getting there and we were the only white people on the bus, obviously westerners never went to that part it was all office buildings and what have ye. The café was quite nice, there was other businessmen sitting around talking dead quiet and the owner obviously knew this Mr Carson 'cos he gave us a table in the corner quite cosy for having a serious aul yarn, the whole thing reminded me of doing deals back home except I'd no piece on me this time. Olly was a bit nervous and over-enthusiastic, I was glad I was there just to watch his back sure there were two fellas sitting smoking cigarettes at another table looking over at us from behind their mirrored sunglasses. I knew straightaway they must of been Carson's goons keeping an eye on proceedings, Olly was so worked up he never even noticed them.

Carson ordered coffee for the three of us and gave me a good looking-over all smiles. So you are seeking work I believe, he goes.

I let Olly do the talking seeing as it was his gig, he mentioned one of his pals who'd escorted fellas from the Middle East into Japan and how highly he'd spoken of Mr Carson and all that sort of blather, yer man Carson just sat there quietly nodding and Olly says to him we wouldn't mind doing something similar but Carson waved his hand and goes, I have a better job than that for you if you are interested.

More money? Olly goes.

Much more, what is the country of origin on your passport?

French, Olly says, and his is UK. That is fine, Carson says, here is what I propose. He had a dead soft accent and his English was good in that menacing sort of polite Singapore way. I will fly you both to Europe and you will be met there by two associates of mine from Pakistan. They will have around twenty passports for each of you. Each passport will be in a different name but will have your photograph. They will also have approximately ten thousand dollars US in traveller's cheques corresponding to the names on the passports, a total of two hundred thousand dollars each. You will spend one month with these men travelling around Europe cashing the cheques, in every country except your home. You will hand the money to my associates every day and spend twenty-four hours in their company. You will not be able to see or talk to anyone else during this period. I am sure you understand the need for security. At the end of this month you will be free to leave and my associates will pay each of you ten per cent of the total sum cashed, which will be approximately twenty thousand dollars, obviously. Simple and clean. All you need to do is handle the transaction of cashing the cheques. There is virtually no risk. We will cover all your expenses.

That sounds really good, Olly starts to say, but I cut him off.

I have a question, I says, yer man gives me a funny

look and then nods, go ahead, he says. What guarantee do we have that we'll get paid at the end of the job?

Olly threw his hands up, oh come on Billy, Mr Carson comes highly recommended we shouldn't.

I wasn't talking to you, I says, be quiet.

Mr Carson gave me an aul thin smile, you have my word, he says.

Right well that's very good, I goes, but I don't know you Mr Carson and the way I'm thinking is that no one knows where we are and what's to stop your associates from Pakistan marching us out into some forest in Denmark or wherever and putting a bullet in our heads rather than hand over the money.

Olly had this look of horror at first but then I see his brow furrowing as he works out what I was saying was entirely possible.

That's not how I do business, Mr Carson goes, consider this a trial and I'm happy with your work then I will give you a much bigger job when you return.

Uh huh, I goes, that's very kind but let me ask you something else, you say there's virtually no risk but I presume these passports are stolen or forged, it seems like if something goes wrong we're the ones who're going to go down for it and you and your associates will just vanish, there's no protection for us at all here.

You ask a lot of questions, Carson goes, starting to look nervous, are you wearing a wire if you're recording this conversation I will deny everything, do you work for Interpol?

Whoa hold your horses there, I says, calm down, do I look like the sort of cunt works for Interpol, this is not the movies pal sure we're just a couple of travellers looking to make a wee bit of money, all I'm saying is we have to watch ourselves.

He took the huff then and goes, if you don't want the job that's fine I'll find someone else to do it. I thought you might be interested in making some easy money that's all. So you have my number at the travel agency call me tomorrow and let me know your decision but if I find out you are policemen understand that this will not be good for you. I have many friends in authority here who can make your life very unpleasant.

Aye right no bother, I says, thanks for the coffee Mr Carson we'll give you a ring in the morning. I stood up then and shook his hand I could see the two fellas in the corner watching me like hawks with their hands hovering over the lapels of their jackets sure you could see their pieces bulging a mile off. I had to drag Olly away, as soon as we were outside he was going to start on me but I told him to shut the fuck up and wait until we were well away before he said anything.

There was a bit of a park in the middle of this aul roundabout so we ran over there to sit down in the sun. Come on then, I says, let's hear it.

Are you mad, he goes, what the fuck's your problem this is a golden opportunity. Mr Carson's well connected and you're pissing him off already, he's right this is easy money. I didn't think you'd be scared after all you've done.

Is that what you think, I says, that I'm feared? Aye well maybe you're right I'm just sayin' we'd be the lowest rung on the ladder here and totally expendable sure for all intents and purposes we're just a couple of drifters and they'd save forty grand just by walking away at the end never mind the fact they might put the two of us in a shallow grave just to keep our gobs shut, don't tell me you're actually considering this, have you no sense?

Actually what I was thinking, he says, was that we could deal with the two Pakistanis and take the whole lot two hundred grand each and disappear.

I laughed then, aye brilliant idea a couple of hard cases from Pakistan sure we'll just tie them up and do a runner to Argentina dead easy are you off your fucking head sure we've no idea who we're working for here could be the Triads or the Russians or worse. Even if we could pinch the money sure we'd be looking over our shoulders the rest of our lives it's bad enough now I don't want to be looking at every Pakistani wondering if he's going to pull out a machete and chop my fucking arms off, the whole thing stinks so it does.

Olly flopped back on the grass with his arms over his head and an aul scowl on his face. He could see the sense in what I was saying, he just didn't want to believe it. *Putain*, he goes, thumping the grass with his fist. I thought we could do this thing together you and me make some money and have a good time.

Sorry brother, I says, count me out sure I'm fed up with this life-on-the-run business.

So what you going to do, he says, work in an office settle down and get married, look at yourself in the mirror sometime Billy *sérieusement*.

I know, I says, you think I don't know how it goes sitting on some train or bus on the way to work every morning the same aul faces no talk reading the celebrity news in the paper, every cunt worried sick about the mortgage or the credit card bill or the repayments on their fucking piece-of-shit Toyota Corolla big ball of fucking knots in their guts an aul feeling of dread sitting on their shoulders destroying them before the day's even begun. You think I don't know about that life I seen it all around me everywhere I go, fuck sake people standing in the queue at the supermarket or at the hole in the wall or at the bus stop in the fucking freezing rain or in the dole office. You think I don't know what the world's like sure I seen more than most men could stand and I done things I'm not proud of, the only way I could get out was to touch the face of fucking Heaven on a Friday night, pills and trips and dust and fighting and drink and sticking my knob in every wet hole I could find knowing there was millions of others out there who felt just like I did, that's what I depended on because I knew there might not be a tomorrow and the soundtrack in my head was the only thing made it all bearable sure if you could only hear it you'd know what I mean.

I can't do it no more Olly, I can't keep running when all I'm doing is trying to run from myself and I can't be involved in any passport scams or wild money-making schemes. I done enough bad shit in my life and I need to get myself sorted out before it's too late, maybe it is already maybe I'm just kidding myself on but I got nothing left no more enthusiasm for nothing I've just got to stop and face up to the world before it crushes me like the fucking worthless bug that I am.

That was about it between me and the Frenchman. Sure he said I was having a meltdown and I says, aye well it's about time, I mean it's not like I burst into tears or nothing. I know I keep saying how what I done's going to fuck me up but it's not that bad, like yer man Sigmund Freud said psychotherapy works on every cunt except the Irish who don't seem to need it. I mean I was all right I could still function and go about my business and have a laugh and that, I just needed to have a good look at myself and square everything away in my head so's I could get on with things and maybe work out what the fuck I was going to do with myself.

I could see the years stretching out ahead and there wasn't much future for an aul Orangeman thug outside of his natural environment so to speak. I had the chance to leave all that shite behind and I was only now realising after all this time that I'd sort of fallen into that dead young or was pushed whatever way you want to look at it but I could do anything I wanted within reason, I wasn't stupid or nothing I mean no genius either but I wasn't a lost cause yet, that's what I'm saying.

That's what I tried to tell Olly, I think he understood but he wasn't ready to be going down that road himself just yet sure he had the spirit of adventure or whatever in him.

The last I seen of him was when he jumped on a bus for the Cambodia, he heard it was even cheaper over there and not ruined yet by tourists like the Thailand was. He didn't know what he was going to do other than try to shag loads of wee Khmer girls and he said cheerio to me in the middle of a busy street it was about eight o'clock at night and dead warm, he was all cheerful to be embarking on another adventure but I was a wee bit cut up though I didn't show it.

He gave me a big hug and says, *T'inquiète pas Billy, l'avenir te trouvera!* I knew the first part was don't worry Billy but the rest was a bit beyond me so I shouts what was that as he was clambering on the bus with his aul filthy rucksack over one shoulder. He disappeared for a minute getting himself a seat I suppose and then just as the bus goes to pull away he leans out the door and gives me a wave laughing like a madman, the future will find you, he shouts, pumping his fist in the air and whooping and then he was gone.

Even though he was a bit of a cunt I liked our Olly and I was sorry I couldn't be more fun for him, he was one of those lads out there doing his own thing and not worrying about tomorrow or the next day sure you have to admire that. I felt dead weird after he was gone sure that was me on my own again, he was about the closest thing to a friend I had and I'd no idea when I'd ever see him again, maybe never.

'Cos I was feeling miserable I checked out of the shitehole we were in and got myself a room at the Sheraton, it was expensive but fucking lovely, I just wanted a bit of luxury before going on my way. I went shopping too and got myself some new gear clothes and a rucksack that didn't stink of monkey shite, a CD Walkman too and a bunch of aul albums. I got Oasis Tricky Leftfield Faith No More Chemical Brothers, fucking magic so it was listening to good music again.

I called up the contact I'd been thinking about, this aul fella who'd been recommended me by Big Jim just in case I ever needed an out. Milan was his name, he was Croatian and he'd done identity work with Big Jim for years before doing a runner, something about the war over there, sure I never pried, best not to with men like that. God knows who he was really. He'd been living in Thailand for years sure he was even married to one of the locals and had a couple of kids. I'd met him once before and stayed at his place down the coast for a couple of days when I first flew in but he had a car rental business in Bangkok too, it was supposed to be a front but I think he enjoyed it more than doing forgeries. Anyway he never done much anymore but he was glad to hear from me and said he'd sort me out with a new passport and a bank account and everything, he didn't ask no questions about where I was going or nothing sure he'd more sense but I told him it wasn't urgent anyway I wasn't in trouble with the peelers or nothing.

That makes it easy, he says, have you decided on a new name?

I had to think about it for a minute. I didn't want to change it too much 'cos that would be a pain, then I 'membered the song Tanya played for me back on the island 'Summertime' and how her favourite singer was Ella Fitzgerald so I says to Milan I says, I want to keep William 'cos that's my real name but change Montgomery to Fitzgerald. Billy Fitzgerald, he goes, that sounds all right, no not Billy, I says, I want to leave Billy behind when I was a wean my granda used to call me Will before he passed on and I think I'll start using that instead.

Will it is, Milan goes, I'll have it couriered over to the Sheraton in a day or two and get your money transferred to a new account in that name though that might take a few weeks, you should go for a holiday in the meantime.

A holiday, I says, sure my whole life's a fucking holiday it's time to move on.

Whatever you say Will, he goes, it was weird hearing it but I'd have to get used to it. Billy Montgomery was almost dead now and Will Fitzgerald was coming out of the womb all sticky and covered in goo. I'd high hopes for the lad sure he couldn't do any worse than his father.

The plan was to get the fuck out of Asia and stay well away from Europe sure I never wanted to go back there unless I had to like if someone died or I was accepting the Nobel Prize or something. That didn't leave too many places that spoke English and the only person I knew and got on with was Tanya out in Australia so I decided to take her up on the offer of heading down to Cairns. I didn't want to impose too much on the girl and it's not like I expected her to shack up with me or nothing. I just figured I'd go for a wee visit and get a feel for the place and then maybe just stay there and go to night school or something and learn a trade if the money ran low sure I could always get a job labouring or whatever, that's what all the thick Paddies do anyway. The point was it'd be a new start for me far from the old country and that was where I wanted to be, as far away as possible from them cunts. I fully intended never to contact Big Jim or any of them ones ever again Australia was going to be my clean slate and Will Fitzgerald would be the new man I'd become.

I was sitting by the pool letting all this sink in drinking a mai tai wearing my new shorts and a nice wee short-sleeved shirt that covered my aul tattoos. I didn't know what I was going to do about them, seeing NO SURRENDER backwards in the mirror everyday was doing my head in a bit. I was thinking maybe I could get them removed in Australia or cover them up with something a bit less aggressive when this middle-aged fella came over and sat at the next table. He was going bald on top and he looked like an eejit but dead relaxed, probably on a business trip or something I was thinking likely just had his knob sucked by some wee slip of a thing upstairs.

I was totally wrong about him though, he says bout ye how's it going, sure I couldn't believe it he was from back home and I reached for my back pocket looking for a piece the first thing I thought was fuck me he's here to rub me out probably a Provo hitman, course I'd no piece on me and I starts looking around to see where the rest of his team was but there was only a couple of aul ladies sitting drinking tea not yer typical kill squad.

Fucking paranoid as fuck I realised then, calm yourself down Billy I mean Will I says to myself, aye not bad, I goes to him, what about yourself. His eyes lit up then, are you from Northern Ireland, he goes, I don't believe it.

Aye, I says, been a while since I lived there but I'm a Belfast boy what about you.

He sits up then all smiles, unbelievable, he goes, sure it's a small aul world isn't it though. I'm from Larne, Tony Baird's the name pleased to meet ye.

I shook his hand and said the words for the first time, Will Fitzgerald, he squinted then, I could see him thinking it was a bit strange 'cos William's a Prod name and Fitzgerald's a Fenian one but he took it in his stride and goes, can I join you for a drink?

No bother, I goes, come on ahead sure what'll ye have.

What's that you're drinking with the umbrella in it, he says, don't tell us you're an aul knob jockey no offence like but my bap's not buttered on that side.

I laughed then sure his sense of humour was like mine, straightaway I 'membered what it was like back home with the constant craic. Are ye not, I says, sure I'm disappointed when I saw those shorts you're wearing I thought sure you were an arse bandit like me.

He screwed his face up then and started to laugh, no rusty sheriff's badge on me, he says, though maybe you're a deputy yourself. Talking to him was just what I needed, a bloody good aul laugh for a change.

I got the drinks in and says to him, what's the craic then Tony you out here on business or something, aye he goes, boring as fuck sure I won't do your head in with it needless to say I work for a big accountancy firm and they've got an office out here sure they sent me out for a conference I don't know why, they must of wanted rid of me for the week but I'm not complaining.

Accountancy, I says, aye right that seems to be popular out here you must be good with the numbers then I suppose, aye he says, always was my da had a Spar in Larne and I used to help him out with the books when I was a wean so it made sense to do it at uni.

Did you go to Queen's then, I says, nah he goes, any excuse to get out of Northern Ireland sure I went to Aberdeen to get away from all that sectarian shite you know what I mean?

Totally, I goes, shifting in my seat to make sure he couldn't see my Loyalist tattoos. I don't blame ye, I wish I'd paid more attention in school and fucked off out of there myself.

He looked at me funny then, sure you're only a young man, he goes, you could get yourself on a course somewhere no bother I'm sure.

Aye I was thinking that, I says, I wonder what I'd like doing.

Well what are you good at, he goes.

I let out a big sigh then, aye good question sure the only A-levels I could of done would of been eating, sleeping and wanking.

Right, he laughs, well what do you like then what're your interests?

I was a bit embarrassed, well I like reading books, I says but that's a recent development since I come over here. To tell you the truth Tony I'm not exactly blessed in the brains department, I'm the first one to admit it.

Don't put yourself down, he goes, sure it takes most people years to work out what they're going to do with themselves I was lucky I knew from a young age you've plenty of time don't worry about it, just relax and keep reading that's my advice.

We talked for ages he was quite chilled out so he was, not what you'd expect from an accountant from Larne or any cunt from the province for that matter, sure I'd never met a middle-aged man from Northern Ireland who wasn't twisted with bitterness.

Here, he goes, have you tried Vipassana yet, I don't know, I says, is it like the Chang 'cos I'm sick of that.

No, he goes, it's not a beer you dunderhead it's a

meditation retreat in the jungle.

What do you mean, I says, like yoga and that?

Aye well that's part of it, he goes, but the idea is you go to some isolated place run by Buddhists and you live like they do for ten days not saying nothing and just thinking about things.

It sounds like a bunch of aul hippie nonsense, I says, you mean you don't say nothing at all?

Not a word, he goes, silent retreat just contemplation.

Have you been, I says.

Aye sure I've been twice now, once up in Chang Mai and another time down the coast it was brilliant so it was. I come out of it feeling a hundred and ten per cent.

Honest, I says, is it that good, well it's hard work too, he goes, you have to get up at four in the morning and you can go a bit mad not being able to talk but if you've any aul problems weighing you down sure you've nothing else to do but confront them, it's not for everyone but I'd personally recommend it I'd be a lot more messed up if I hadn't done it my older brother got killed by the Provos when I was young, mistaken identity you know the sort of thing two boys with balaclavas on walked into the bar and shot him in the face they thought he was an off-duty policeman, it played on me for a long time but I put it to bed and made my peace after becoming a Buddhist.

What, I says, you're a Buddhist, fuck me are you a Catholic Buddhist or a Protestant one?

He cracked up laughing then, that's hilarious, he goes,

aye, I says, sure I'm only kidding on. I wasn't at all it was a serious question but as soon as I said it I realised how fucking stupid it was. With a name like Baird he was obviously Protestant.

Is there a Buddhist church in Larne, I says, he thought that was funny too, if there was it'd be a congregation of one, he says, nah look I'm not into all that sectarian stuff like I said I've opened my mind to new things now sure the world's too big to be worrying about all that nonsense, like a muppet I used to think once you'd seen the Mountains of Mourne and been over to Magaluf that was about it. Back home they'd have you believe Northern Ireland was the be-all end-all and when you're there the problems we have seem like the most important thing in the world but as soon as you step outside the country you realise it's a load of aul bollocks, so it is. No one cares about the place. You tell people and they've not even heard of it. There's too much to see and do in the world to be pinching your head with that aul Catholic and Protestant codswallop.

My mind was racing at what he was saying, sure I'd a couple of weeks spare until my new bank account got sorted out and the fact that the idea of doing his retreat thing scared me a wee bit made me think I should do it. He was a good lad our Tony and quite diplomatic too, he knew I must of been in trouble back home sure he probably put two and two together but he kept his mouth shut and didn't preach or nothing, just said I should try the meditation thing and see if it did me any good, couldn't do any harm and if I didn't like it sure I could leave any time I wanted.

What sort of people go on it then, I says, are they all fucked up, sure you wouldn't believe some of the stories, he goes, you get to talk at the end and find it all out the worst part of it is the women though.

How so, I says, well they're gorgeous so they are, he goes, and there's loads of them right there in front of ye but you can't talk to them, you shouldn't even be looking at them but it's hard and you're not supposed to touch yourself either so you can imagine.

Fuck me, I says, it sounds like being a monk for a fortnight, it is, he goes, sure the one down the coast is in a monastery right on the edge of the jungle, pack your robes if you're going.

Well I wouldn't mind trying it to be honest with you Tony, I goes, but I don't have any robes or nothing, sure where do you buy them?

I'm only messing ye, he says, just go the way you are, the monks wear the robes not you, dunderhead.

The aul cocktails fairly flowed after that sure Tony had an expense account and everything, he was putting it all on the bill of his company back home and it wasn't long before the two of us were spackered. He was great craic, so he was. Him and me near drunk the bar dry and fell about in the pool and chatted up the ladies, a good aul blowout was just what I needed after seeing off the Frenchman.

He had hollow legs on him too our Tony, sure he was

still staggering by the end of the night and had to carry me back to the room. I was slurring my words trying to tell him he was brilliant and if I'd been a knob jockey sure he'd be the man for me right enough and the accountancy wasn't boring at all and if anyone said any different he should let me know and I'd burst them. The last thing I 'member was collapsing onto the bed, CDs flying all over the place, thinking what a laugh I was going to try my hand at being a monk.

Tony was taking a slash in the bathroom and I gulders at him, hey Obi Wan Kenobi, show us your lightsaber. He laughed and shouted something back but sure I didn't hear it I was already curled up in the crisp sheets, halfway to nirvana.

It was weird checking into a monastery so it was, a bit like a hotel only there's no room service no cable TV not even a bed actually. I had a cell sort of thing, a square made out of stone with an aul door hanging off the hinges, totally featureless inside except for a slab of concrete with a wooden board stuck to it sure that was the bed hard as fuck and the pillow was even more of a laugh, a wee block of wood like a brick with a bevel cut out of it. The only way to get any sleep at all was to lie flat on your back and work your neck into the dip in the block. I would of complained to the management only I'd signed an agreement on the way in to say I'd keep my mouth shut for the next ten days and my sign language wasn't up to scratch.

This tough-looking monk signed me up, his face and

his neck was all scarred down one side. I wondered what had happened to him and sure it was only much later I found out a big fucking monkey had clawed the face off of him. Apparently it was well pissed off about something, gone loco on the rampage foaming at the mouth and had come down into the local village, everyone was dead scared. It was going spastic, it tried to grab a wean but this fella wrestled it to the ground only not before it had give him an aul beating. I was dead impressed when I heard that, sure monkeys are strong bastards, I wouldn't like to fight one anyway.

So the deal was once you were signed in and paid up you were given a cell of your own in this block of about fifty. It was all fellas but there was another one across the way for women. All you had to do was keep your cell clean and sign up for a chore you had to do every day, most of them were already gone the good ones anyway like cleaning the bogs and emptying the scorpion bucket, so I chose the one no cunt wanted which was to give a reading from their Bible the Tripitaka halfway through the week in front of everyone. I didn't mind that, it's funny how people would rather clean up shite than talk in public. I'm not bothered by that at all though I laughed when I read that was one of the jobs. Because I was just signing up I could still talk to the monkey monk, he spoke English and everything. Tripitaka, I says, is that not your man from that TV show *Monkey Magic*. He just gave me a look, sorry, I says, no insult intended it's a stupid aul show anyway.

The rest of the day was quiet, nothing to do really but walk around nodding at people 'cos you couldn't say fuck all. They gave you a schedule of what to expect, I didn't like the look of it to be honest. The bells would ring at four in the morning and you had to get up and stagger down to this open-air hall next to a lake to listen to the morning prayer or something and then do some aul yoga whilst the sun came up. Then you'd have breakfast and then back to the hall to listen to some lecture and meditate guided by the monks.

This went on till about lunchtime then you'd eat again and do walking meditation basically that was having a wander and thinking about stuff then one final talk and that was it the rest of the day was your own to do your chores or whatever. There was no eating after lunchtime that didn't sound good but you could go to this hot springs in the evening it was good for your aul legs apparently as they'd be crossed all day and if you weren't used to that it'd be dead sore. Separate baths for the men and the women of course then a wee nighttime lecture and off to bed about nine o'clock.

It sounded like school to me except there was no football or beating people up or snorting whizz behind the bike sheds. Sure I knew fuck all about the Buddhism but I thought why not I'll give it a try sure I'll probably fall asleep getting up at four in the fucking morning. There's a fifty-per-cent drop-out rate yer man says when I signed up, if you don't want to be here or can't follow the rules then it's okay, he goes, just leave don't disturb the others though some people are very into it. Aye no bother, I was thinking, sure it'll be nice having a bit of peace and quiet for a change though ten days doesn't sound hard. I couldn't figure out why people would leave maybe they're so used to talking the silence drives them mad or something.

The grounds of the monastery were quite big and wild it was sort of half in the jungle, there was all kinds of plants and bugs and stuff that I'd never seen before and I was careful not to touch nothing in case I got stung or bit. The monkey monk told me to watch out for snakes they're really bad, he says, cobras especially if one gets in your room run out but don't hurt it, aye right, I was thinking, a fucking cobra sure you'll not see me for dust, worse than the snakes though are the scorpions, he says, don't step on one they're so venomous they kill the cobras. Holy fuck, I thought, isn't it someone's job to empty the scorpion bucket what's that all about, I says to him, we trap them in there at night and release them into the jungle the next day, he says. The Buddhists don't believe in killing nothing not even bugs sure you had to be careful not to step on the ants or swat the mosquitoes, going a bit far I reckoned but he says that might be you in the next life. Right enough, I thought, I'm getting demoted that's for fucking sure. Worst of all, he goes, are the centipedes they're so poisonous they kill the scorpions don't let one get on you. Jesus fuck could they not of built their monastery somewhere where all these creepy crawlies didn't live, I was thinking, when he said there was a fifty-per-cent drop-out rate maybe that was because everyone died or got eaten. What eats the centipedes, I says, we do, he goes, that's what you have for breakfast. He must of seen the look on my face 'cos he burst out laughing then, just a joke, he says, though they might be nice fried.

I quite liked the monkey monk, he spoke well so he did and he was a good laugh, he gave a couple of the talks. I liked his the best 'cos he was hard as fucking nails. I seen him one morning out on the edge of the jungle with his shirt off practising his kung-fu or whatever, fuck me you would not of messed with the cunt he was ripped so he was and had scars all down his side where the monkey had torn him up. He could of taken on twenty men at once like in them martial arts movies he'd fucking kill ye with one punch, I knew a bit of the muaythai and all but he'd knock my bollocks in no doubt about it.

Tony Baird was right about the women. Sure there was fifty of them from all round the world by the looks of it, fucking gorgeous the lot of them too, when they lined up in the food hall to get their rice all the fellas were staring at them with their gobs hanging open. The funny thing was most of the women ignored the lads and sat looking out at the jungle when they were eating whereas the fellas did the opposite and sat looking at the women. The monks had made it quite clear though any fucking around and trying it on with the females and you'd be out on your ear, maybe chucked in the scorpion pit or something beforehand just for good measure.

The main fun for me at the start was trying to guess where everyone was from just by looking at them. There was this dead stern young lad who always wore black T-shirts and shorts and wee square glasses, he looked German to me though he gave me the nod so maybe he thought I was one of his lot, then there was this aul fella about fifty or something in the cell next to mine I thought maybe he was from Eastern Europe, he looked uncomfortable but soldiering on. He waved me over that first night he was pointing at something on the wooden shutter of his window it was a big fuck-off wasp sort of thing with giant wings and a big stinger coming out its arse like a fucking pterodactyl or something so it was, I near swore out loud but just mouthed fuck me instead, he got my meaning all right, have we got a bucket for them I was thinking.

The first night was murder sure but what could you expect it was dead hot in the cell I lay naked on my back on the aul wooden board trying to sleep with my head wedged into their excuse for a pillow, fuck me it was like being tortured or something, you couldn't turn over on your side or nothing 'cos that was too sore. I only slept in fits and starts but at least I got some kip unlike most of the others by the looks of them the next morning. These aul bells started ringing not like church bells back home but more of a low donging sound, quite nice if it wasn't waking ye up at four in the fucking morning sure that's the middle of the night. Anyway I got up I was already awake threw some clothes on and wandered out, there was only about half the fellas up the rest must of been dead to the world, it was like the zombie apocalypse or something seeing everyone drag their heels down to the temple.

Everyone took a spot, we were all in rows the men on one side of the hall the women on the other, there was more of them than there was of us now probably about thirty people missing altogether out of the hundred, half of them staggered in a while later but we must of lost fifteen people already that first morning fucking soft cunts get out of your bed there should of been a job kicking people out of their bunks, sure I'd of volunteered for that I'd of made a good sergeant major so I would.

I watched what the others were doing 'cos some of them seemed to know the score, basically you had to sit on the ground with your legs crossed and your back straight your hands resting on your knees, it was all right I didn't mind it sure I was in good shape and all but after an hour my knees and my arse were sore and I had to keep changing sides and stretching my legs out in front of me. Some monk was chanting up the front, it was a bit weird at first but after a while the tones of it relaxed me though I was dying to try it out myself and see if I could make them noises. I noticed pretty much everybody had their eyes closed, a few were nodding off but most seemed to be just concentrating on your man's umming and ahhing up the front. I tried it but when I closed my eyes my mind was buzzing full of stuff I'd done recently going over it and 'membering what I said only saying it better you know the way you do.

I was glad when it ended, I was nodding off too sure I was knackered from not getting much sleep. The sun was just coming up over the horizon, it was dead good seeing the sky turn from black to purple and then red and orange. We had a yoga class then but the teacher wasn't a monk he was one of us that must of been his chore for the week to teach the yoga, it meant he had to speak to explain what he was doing he was American but he says he wanted to speak less every morning as we learned the routine and eventually do the whole thing in silence, aye good luck with that, I was thinking. It went on for an hour and I didn't think I'd be able to 'member all the moves but he was right sure enough by about day four I had it down and so did all the other lads and he was able to shut his gob. Some of the moves were hard even though I was fit as fuck sure I couldn't do them, stretching dead far till you thought your tendons would snap I was sweating so I was. I always thought the yoga was a load of aul hippy shite, no one told me it was a workout. After a couple of days I was dead into it though and practising in my cell sure I could near get my legs behind my head flexible as fuck it turns out, who knew sure I could always find work as a stripper if nothing else worked out.

I was never so happy to get breakfast in me sure I was starving, it was just vegetables and rice but it tasted lovely so it did all washed down with soy milk served to ye out of a big vat, it tasted funny but I got used to that too and by the end I loved the stuff they sell it in the 7-Eleven in Bangkok in wee Coke bottles, I was addicted.

There was a big tall monk living there who wasn't Thai at all he was English though he'd been there for donkeys he gave the first lecture all about the Buddhism, it was quite interesting so it was and he was pretty funny the Buddhists seemed to like having a laugh not like the other religions sure it's all fire and brimstone and you're going to Hell for being a cunt, step out of line and you'll get a red-hot poker up your arse. The Buddhists were different, they just had this sort of aye whatever attitude don't worry about the future or the past sure where are you right now. I liked that so I did sure that was more like how I'd been living anyway not knowing where I was going in life and not worrying about it too much, it was the big unknown for me sure I didn't have a clue. The past was my problem but your man talked about that too it was a bit of a worry for me given all I'd done but sure everybody's got things they want to forget, just 'cos mine are a bit fucked up it doesn't make me special or nothing.

Anyway he says doing the meditation was all about focusing your mind on the present and every time you start to imagine what you're going to do next week or what you're going to say to who just snap out of it and come back to the moment, the same if you're dwelling on the past sure that's behind ye and there's fuck all you can do about it so why do your head in worrying about it. Up until lunchtime we all tried it that's when I saw my head was like a non-stop party people running around shouting and screaming music playing and bits of films I'd seen stuff people said to me and girls sweat dripping off of their tits it was fucking mayhem so it was pure chaos like no sense to it at all and amongst it was all the bad stuff wee snippets that jumped to the foreground now and then of me knocking the fuck out of some Catholic lad tied to a chair or someone falling in a crowd after getting hit in the head by a brick I'd chucked or the sound of a drill bit going through some poor cunt's kneecap and worst of all I mean scary as fuck puts all the rest to shame was the face of our Mark lying on the cobblestones.

I had to snap out of it and lie back on the ground for a bit. I was soaked with sweat and my heart was pounding in my chest, holy fuck I was thinking this is wild worse than any drug I don't know if I'm going to make it through this no wonder half the people drop out. I calmed myself down thinking come on Billy I mean Will sure you're a hard cunt you can take it. I knew that was true at least. I looked around from where I was lying and there must of been about ten people sobbing fucking hardcore the Buddhism I was thinking this enlightenment stuff better be worth it.

The aul walking meditation was the hardest for me sure I just couldn't concentrate you were supposed to pick a wee strip of grass and pace back and forth dead slow and I mean like you're walking in slow motion or something, fuck me I was thinking if anyone could see the lot of us ninety-odd people with one foot in the air they'd think it was the ministry of funny walks or something. I tried it again and again but it just struck me as dumb so I gave up and went for a wander instead, the monk said you could do that if you weren't into it there was plenty to see and gawk at so just dander around observing sort of thing looking at all the wee details the bounty of nature or whatever.

I quite liked doing that actually though I couldn't do the meditation at the same time, I had to be sitting down concentrating for that but it was good stretching the aul sore knees. There was all sorts of bugs and creepy crawlies to look at I didn't know what half of them were, flying things and worms with funny colours on their backs and an orange spider inside this aul log waiting for his lunch to come along, the place was alive so it was but my favourite was the ants I could watch them all day. I followed their trail sure it was about a mile long they must of had some serious business to attend to, there was a million of the wee cunts going along in a line some of them were carrying wee bits of leaves the hard workers obviously, I don't know what the rest were up to going to or from their work I suppose. Fuck they're amazing so they are in a world of their own they don't give a fuck about us humans and our aul problems, they've got attitude too this big red one crawled past me I was sitting on the ground watching them and he must of seen me or something, the wee bastard stops and looks right up at me as if to say what the fuck do you want fuck off out of here or I'll bite ye. I'm about a thousand times his size or something, I could crush him no bother and he still comes at me all threatening like did you not hear me get to fuck. I jumped up thinking, aye all right pal take it easy I'm going now. I had to sit somewhere else and hope he didn't come back, the wee fucker set of balls on him like.

By the time evening come and the hot springs was on the menu I was raring to go the place was supposed to chill you out but I was full of beans so I was, I felt quite good about everything and I wanted to have an aul craic with the lads but it was frustrating sure you couldn't say nothing. Anyway the hot springs was just a big pit in the ground you could only get about a dozen people in there at once, it wasn't very big but it was boiling so it was and dead salty sure you could float on your back no bother if there was room. All these dead-serious-looking cunts were in there you know the type westerners that think because they're into the eastern mysticism and all that they're better than everybody looking down at ye as if to say I'm on a higher plain than you or something. I reckoned they'd missed the point completely sure the monk said Buddhists treated everyone equal I felt like slapping a few lugs but instead I done a few laps of the pool like I said it wasn't very big and it wasn't made for swimming but I didn't care I had to get rid of some energy. The serious cunts were all looking at me like I shouldn't of been swimming 'cos that was against the rules or something I was meant to just sit there contemplating the universe sure I'd been doing that all day. I went back and forth a few times fuck it was hot and then your man from the cell next door to me arrives with a big smile on his face I was glad to see him, at least he seemed not to be taking everything so seriously. He lowered himself in and goes, ooh ahh at the heat of it and the others all glared at him like you're not supposed to make any sounds 'cos that's breaking your vow of silence, fuck me I was thinking, leave him alone sure if you got bit on the arse by one of them centipedes I'd like to see ye keeping quiet then sure you'd be jumping around going fuck me, where's the doctor, get me a helicopter, fucking hurry up.

Anyway your man next door nods at me smiling and watches me swimming for a bit then taps me on the shoulder and waves his finger not like telling me off or nothing but with a look of concern on his face like watch yourself it's a bit hot for that. Him and me were getting a good non-verbal understanding I don't know why but I nods back thanks at him and climbed out, I'd had enough anyway. I walked back towards the cells it was a warm night and as I was walking I started sweating and getting dizzy fuck me I was thinking I'm going to pass out here so I hurried up back to my one-bunk Hilton.

As soon as I got in I had to lie down on the stone floor I was burning up my temperature went through the roof the sweat was literally pouring off me into a puddle on the ground. Stupid bastard, I was thinking, what'd ye swim in that hot water for now you're fucked I was worried for about five minutes that I was melting or at least that I'd done some damage to myself overheated the aul ticker or something. Thank fuck the floor was just concrete and quite cold that cooled me down so it did, I lay there for about half an hour until it was safe to get up my legs were dead wobbly and I drunk about a litre of water straight down so I wouldn't die of the dehydration the floor was soaking so it was. Don't be swimming in the hot springs in future I told myself you're not at fucking Club Med here.

No wonder some burst into tears their first day, sure

by day three I was in trouble myself. The only thing that was keeping me from drowning in my own head was exercising and doing the yoga and that, even when we were meant to be resting I done it just to keep my mind off of things. You know how there's those films like *The Poseidon Adventure* where some big ocean liner gets caught in a storm out to sea and the whole thing gets turned upside down and people are falling all over the place and getting killed and there's only a couple of aul survivors the usual types, an action man to lead them out a sexy woman some aul couple who're not gonna make it and maybe a dog or something. Well that's what it was like inside my noggin all upside down shite flying everywhere the whole thing disorientating only there was no Gene Hackman to sort it all out, fuck sake where's the Hackman when you need him?

It got so that every time I closed my aul peepers and concentrated on the circular breathing like yer man says to do I'd suddenly find myself somewhere in the past, it was weird so it was it was like I was there just watching the younger version of me. Good-looking cunt not as many tattoos or scars bit skinnier too sure I put the beef on once I started hitting the gym not to mention the Fenian punch bags we strung up like sides of meat. It was so realistic a couple of times I felt like putting my arm around his shoulders and pulling him aside to give him a wee bit of advice, fuck if only we could do that eh sure I'd go back and clip myself round the lugs and stop me from hurting people.

I seen things I'd buried and thought I'd never 'member, they come up like fucking zombies climbing out of the grave. I'm talking times when I was a wee lad knocking about the Shankill estate playing football with the goals painted on the gable wall, there was no grass or nothing and there'd always be some cunt who would come along and take our ball some older lad and if ye gave him any aul lip he'd burst ye. That was how I got noticed by Big Jim and them sure I was a skinny wee fucker but I wouldn't take no shit, I knocked the fuck out of this kid about five years older than me and about twice my size, he had me down on the ground and was whaling on me but it was just making me madder. I near bit his finger off, I don't know where the strength came from but I knocked him off of me and stood up dead quick and stomped on his knees as hard as I could so he couldn't get up and batter me no more.

My granda used to say, go for the knees Billy, it doesn't matter how big they are kick any man in the knee and he'll go down like a ton of bricks and then he's yours for the taking. He'd fought in the war my granda hard as fuck like not like my da who just worked in the factory and kept his head down it was obvious who I took after. Granda had scars all over him like I do now from knives and bullets, he'd been shot five times by the Japanese in Burma but they couldn't kill him.

When I was eight he told me about this time he was on patrol in the jungle and him and his mates ran into the enemy like walked right into them sort of thing everyone had their rifles over their shoulders so it was hand-to-hand combat game on fucking wild so it was he said, one of the Japanese fellas had a fucking sword and was going all samurai chopping off arms and legs. Anyway he ran my granda through with it he was dead lucky though it went through his shoulder or something missed the vital organs granda fell back and the sword stuck in the ground on the other side of him. The Japanese fella was going to pull it out and finish him off but granda grabbed his arm he was dead strong so he was, he made him hold the sword in there 'cos he had no other weapon and while he was leaning over trying to pull it out granda drew his knife out of his belt calm as you like and stuck it in the side of the cunt's head, right in the brainpan he told me. Yer man couldn't believe it, Granda said he breathed his last with a look of shock on his face like how could this pasty Irish cunt with ginger hair have defeated him a fucking big-shot samurai, just goes to show ye like.

Anyway it was about the time my granda died that I started going off the rails so to speak I was ten and it cut me up so it did sure I loved him, he had an aul budgie that used to fly around the room and perch on his head and sometimes it shit down his neck but he didn't care. He told me all the war stories my da didn't want to hear, about running round the jungle with the Ghurkhas, sure they didn't even carry guns they were so tough just them big curved knives, they'd sneak up on the Japanese and slit their throats just for fun. He didn't like authority neither but kept getting promoted 'cos he survived battles and he didn't want to be an aul officer so he'd punch some senior cunt in the gob and get busted back down to private.

Hearing the stories I just wanted to be there with him, my da was a different kettle of fish entirely a good man like just not interested in much, a bit boring to be honest. Suppose having a war hero for yer da wasn't the best, Granda was probably tough on him but he thought I was the bee's knees. The aul malaria used to come back on him in later years and sure all his pals had been killed or if they come back they were fucked up so he sat in his room drinking stout most of the time, I think he was just glad of my company.

Heart attack got him like so many, hard as fuck to the end though my granny said she found him doing push-ups in the lounge before he collapsed, died in the ambulance of course. Something about the way he died made an impression on me so it did, he must of known he was having a heart attack so what was he doing push-ups for? To try and fight it off or to bring it on, either way how many 75-year-olds do you know that can do push-ups at the best of times never mind during a fucking heart attack. One tough aul bastard so he was.

Doing the meditation I could see now how I ended up under Big Jim's influence sure I was just looking for someone to show me the way. My da should of stepped in but he was too busy aspiring to some sort of middle-class life out of the gutter. Fair enough you might say wanting something better for his weans than what his own da gave him spending years off at the war and then all changed when he came back as a hardcore fucking killer but all the same what a load of aul pish, I mean catch yourself on there's no room for middle class in Belfast there's either poor as fuck or rich as fuck and the rest get preyed on by both. I know where I'd rather be at one end or the other, never in the middle no way.

Aye so it was all starting to become clear in my head what had happened and what a stupid cunt I'd been only of course I was young and impressionable so there's not much I could of done about it. Big Jim had me and some other kids Johnny Robinson and them ones running about doing wee jobs for him, not much at first just delivering packages and messages. I done a good job sure I was dead sneaky and if any peelers pulled me up I'd say nothing only go fuck yourselves get your hands off me you bunch of cunts.

Fucking talk about misplaced loyalty I didn't know what I was doing sure I'd of done anything Big Jim asked and did too. He had me climb a lamppost one time and run chicken wire across the street then when the army come round patrolling and some young soldier was sticking out the top of the Saracen he'd not see the wire and get decapitated. I 'member watching it and saying holy fuck did you see that to the other lads, blood was spurting out the neck and the arms was flailing about the head rolled down the back of the tank and onto the road then we darted out and kicked it around like a football before running off. I can't even imagine why we were doing that sure the Brits were supposed to be on our side but Big Jim didn't give a fuck it was just like a test thing to see if we'd do it and sure even if we got caught what could they say who done it who cut that poor bastard's head off, a bunch of kids?

I hadn't thought about that day in years but when I was sitting in the temple it flashed before me like I was there standing right beside Big Jim as he watched us run out into the diesel fumes of the armoured vehicle to kick some nineteen-year-old's severed head, a wee sly grin on his face as he took a drag on his cigarette. Can you imagine being in that tank when your pal's body falls down in beside ye with no head on it squirting blood all over ye? I mean fuck me. Fuck me.

Like yer man said after a couple of days the numbers started to dwindle, people going mad I suppose with whatever was in their head and not being able to talk about it or just not sleeping on the aul wooden boards or used to getting their dinner at night and not liking being hungry sure it was no picnic but what the fuck did they expect, Euro Disney? Bunch of soft cocks I reckoned sure how many of them would of had stuff like mine to deal with, round about zero like no messing, I hope so anyway.

Apart from doing the yoga all the time to give myself wee goals like seeing if I could bend over backwards and do yon bridge manoeuvre the other thing keeping me from going off my rocker was looking at the women. There was no bikini action or nothing sure that wasn't allowed so you had to use your imagination. The more I looked though the more I realised I'd been beholden to the fanny for a long time it was like my church or something sure I kneeled down and worshipped at it my own wee triangular deity like kissing the lips of God so it was.

Still you can't just be thinking about that all the time you have to move on and work things out for yourself never mind about jumping from one bed to the next it's distracting so it is I mean it's brilliant and everything too, I always thought there was no better way to spend your time as a human being than fucking but the problem was I was just using it as a way to distract myself and forget who I was and that's not healthy like. The aul shagging should just be part of your life not the be-all end-all not the whole point of your existence, I mean you shouldn't be wandering around just thinking who am I going to stick my knob in next aye her over there she'll do right very good that was brilliant love now who's next. It's madness living like that so it is sure there's no end to it the ultimate loneliness is not when you're fucking no one at all sure it's when you're trying to fuck everyone.

Hard habit to break though when you're totally addicted but I was thinking maybe I should just try admiring women and learning from them like with Tanya rather than just imagining them in the buff with their arse in the air though fuck me that's a tricky image to shake, not entirely unpleasant you know what I mean like. Anyway the aul meditation was clearing my head a wee bit on these matters and so I was trying to put the aul rampant sex stuff to the back of my mind and not let it dominate me focus on myself and working out who the fuck I was for a change instead, it was a bit of a relief actually, like lifting a breeze block off of your shoulders something was changing inside me sure I could tell that even though I wasn't sure what the fuck it was, maybe not good. I didn't know nothing else to do but ride it out and see where I ended up after the ten days quite interesting really better than just being the same boring cunt your whole life, right?

It was good just looking at the women after that and appreciating them as something beautiful, a wee nape of the neck here a crooked smile there hair like smoke blowing in the wind I'm no poet or nothing I don't have the words or the sense to be able to describe what I was seeing but you know there's something humbling about being in the presence of beauty and not just wanting to debase it, this was a new thing for me. For the first time in my life I had this weird feeling down in my gut when I looked at people sort of warm and I hesitate to say this but kinda happy like being on a pill or something only not wanting to dance to Paul Oakenfold.

It was like I felt love for my fellow man sort of thing, fuck me that sounds dead embarrassing just as well I couldn't say nothing though you could tell from the way some of the others carried themselves that they were feeling it too. My neighbour the aul fella sure I could tell he was dying to give me a hug.

The worst was this redhead. Fuck me she was just

about the most gorgeous thing I'd ever seen on the planet like she was from somewhere else I don't know people say angels but that's dead cheesy so it is and I don't believe in all that shite anyway but I could see why people say it 'cos there's no words in our language to describe someone like that when you see them. Apart from the long straight red hair her skin was pale but covered in freckles I suppose she had to watch out for the sun, she always wore this loose white blouse thing and a pair of fisherman pants, your classic spiritual backpacker sort of get-up.

I'd seen her wandering around looking at the plants and bugs like I done except the smile on her face could of ended wars. I gave her a wide berth 'cos I didn't want to be fixating on her or freaking her out or nothing but it was hard not to keep glancing over at her in the temple. It was a good aul test of my resolve not to think about fanny all the time, every time I started undressing her in my mind I threw a bucket of freezing-cold water over myself mentally like and concentrated on something else like an ant walking on the ground or something.

When I first started noticing her because she was a ginger my first thought was fuck no she must be Irish sure that's all I need but the more I looked I couldn't believe she was one of ours sure they don't make them like that back home or if they do it's not long until they've got an aul pinched face from squinting against the rain and the bullshit. Hers was all soft and open and wide-eyed obviously not from back home but I couldn't figure out where the fuck she was from, it was good fun wondering though in the end I decided it must be some planet orbiting a sun far from our wee candle and she was just visiting us primitive humans for a laugh or to write an article for the *Proxima Centauri Guardian* about what dickheads we were.

It was funny being dead quiet all the time and only hearing the sounds of birds and the monks and the aul donging bells. I was glad I'd picked the chore I did, in the end it was about day four when I had to read something out from the Tripitaka. The tough monk with the monkey scars gave me a bit of paper with the words on it that I had to read the day before so's I could go through it and make sure I didn't fuck it up or nothing.

It was a good wee story about a king telling this fella to round up all the blind people in the town and try explaining to them what an elephant was by letting them touch bits of it but then when he asked the blind what the elephant was like they all said something different 'cos they'd touched different parts, it was one of them fables basically saying that every fucker sees things different and no one's got a fucking clue what the truth of the matter is really that's what I took out of it anyway, sure I'd met loads of cunts back home who thought they knew the score but they'd no idea.

Anyway I had to go up the front and read it out, I was a wee bit nervous but not too bad even though everyone was watching me. It was dead early in the morning still dark and lots of tired-looking faces but sure they all perked up when I started talking. I hammed it up a bit, exaggerating the words and that sort of like a performance or something sure it was obvious everyone was all starved of entertainment 'cos they started laughing dead quick at my antics. It was weird hearing my voice and I suppose some were thinking fuck me he's from Belfast and others were probably thinking what sort of fucking stupid accent is that like but at least I was talking proper 'cos I was reading something out and not just speaking like I normally do a mile a minute and catch yourself on and away and fuck you're a head-the-ball and all that stuff.

Those who had been shown the ear of the elephant replied, the elephant your majesty is just like a winnowing basket, I says, now that's not even funny or nothing but sure they were cracking up maybe it was the way I said it, you can never tell with an Irish accent this one time a Welsh girl went gaga over me saying washing-up liquid, what's that all about? Anyway I had the crowd in the palm of my hand and I felt like Dave Allen or someone telling dirty jokes down the comedy club, maybe they were just relieved to hear one of their own talking.

Bit of light relief did the atmosphere a world of good and when I sat back down half the place was staring at me with goofy grins on their faces and the rest of the day I was a minor celebrity people patting me on the back and giving me the nod. The best part was all the women looking at me like he's brilliant so he is I wouldn't mind getting into his fisherman pants. Fuck me I tried not to think about it especially the redhead who was giving me sultry looks, don't tell us she fancies me I was thinking sure if we get together after this it'll be like a thermonuclear explosion.

It was a good day though, not a single person there wished me any ill will they were all looking friendly at me and smiling, a bit strange for a Prod from the Shankill Road when you're used to everyone hating your guts and wanting to take a baseball bat with a nail in it to your knees. I went to bed quite happy that night thinking this is all right maybe I can get through this sure I'm halfway there and quite enjoying it, there's something to be said for the aul Buddhism.

Weird stuff started to happen when I was doing the aul meditation. Like yer man said I just concentrated on my breathing going in a circle and didn't think about the past no more all that noise and chaos in my head was fading away into the background it was getting quiet in there and I started seeing this vision sort of thing, I don't know how to describe it. It was like a wee gentle dream only I was awake maybe in a trance or something I don't know anyway here's the thing, in it I was floating in the ocean but the waves were dead calm and all was quiet, I wasn't worried about nothing just floating there with my mouth shut and not a thought in my head. The sea below was deep and dark, I couldn't see nothing down there but I wasn't scared it was like I knew there was sharks and giant squids and piranhas and whatever else lurking in the depths but I knew they wouldn't bother me, I was safe so I was. Away in the distance was a beach with flat land stretching out behind it no trees or buildings or nothing just like a desert but not the Sahara or some place that would kill ye, a friendly patch of land not threatening.

That was it at first, just me hanging out in the middle of nowhere not bothered about being alone. I kept coming back to it though and every time it was a wee bit different, the waves were picking up a bit and carrying me closer to shore or there was other figures floating in the sea as well but too far away for me to see who they were or a couple of white clouds passed overhead or a wee fish came up to have a gander at me and say hello. It was weird as fuck but as the days went by I was thinking ten days wasn't going to be long enough for me and maybe I could take a few days off after, do some talking, get it out of my system and then sign up for another ten if I could or maybe just hang out in the monastery for a while longer not become a monk or nothing I'm not that mad but you know it was obvious this place was changing me for the better, meeting yer man Tony up in Bangkok was maybe the luckiest thing ever happened to me.

The whole thing was coming to an end, those final few days were a blur and I felt like I'd been through the wringer but I'd made it out somehow. I knew it couldn't be all over just like that, there was still the memories of my brother deep down like there'd still be plenty of stuff to come. It helped me start to understand why home was such a toxic fucking place though sure just take my case and multiply it by about a million and try and sort that out, fucking impossible like but one thing was for sure I promised myself there'd be no more aul talk about Fenians and Taigs and Catholics' eyebrows meeting in the middle though that is kinda funny.

I decided to put all that behind me, what a load of shite anyway. I could get angry at Big Jim and them ones that made me that way full of hate and spite but there's no point is there. I was always saying I was a good Prod but the truth of it is I'm not the religious type, I don't really believe in the big man upstairs or anything. I mean if any of that stuff's true sure I'm proper fucked, there'll be a red-hot poker with my name on it down below. Fucking Beelzebub will be rubbing his hands together when he sees me coming.

It's not like I'd seen the light and become an aul Buddhist or something, I mean they seem to have the right idea about not doing no harm to no one and not living in the past or pining after the future that's all good stuff, common sense really. I'm not convinced about the reincarnation or any of that it's believing in stuff you've no idea about that bothers me. I suppose that's what most people call faith but I've no need for it really, sure I can only ever see the world through my own eyes and know my own feelings and thoughts, I don't need to believe in a bunch of aul stories that might be true and might not, be they Christian or Muslim or Buddhist or Jedi or whatever. Aye sure the only thing I know is that

I'm nothing I'm only here for a short time and it doesn't fucking matter in the grand scheme of things, now that maybe frightens some people but not me because the flip side of it is that I'm also everything I'm plugged into the world like there's a lead coming out my arse and going into a big socket and that's brilliant so it is. Aye, there's big questions to be asked who are ye and what are ye doing here and why but you'll never know the answers and that's the whole point really isn't it, that's what it is to be a human being just asking just wondering with an aul cheeky grin on your face.

The final morning I was happy and sad at the same time, it was a bittersweet sort of feeling but when I closed my eyes and tried the meditation the weirdest thing happened, there I was back in the water as usual only the sun was beaming down from the sky not boiling or nothing just warm. I was light as a feather like my weight didn't even matter, I didn't have to paddle to stay afloat and then my legs started to come up from underneath me and I was rising out of the sea floating on the air. I was out of the water completely like a big invisible hand was picking me up.

As I went up I could see the others still down in the water some of them waved to me and I waved back, I felt brilliant I was going higher and higher until their heads were just dots on the surface of the ocean. I could see the beach and the land beyond it wasn't desert at all there was big grass fields and forests and mountains and rivers, it was unbelievable so it was all of nature before me and there was me flying totally light up and up towards the sun until I couldn't feel my body no more that was it that was where it ended I opened my eyes and looked around the temple I was crying a wee bit but not out of sadness or grief but because I was free or maybe close to it.

There was something else though, something I'd glimpsed down there in the water like an aul fucking black monster lurking in the depths. I got a wee flash of an image as I was sitting there rubbing my eyes just a quick one but it was enough. A Doberman pinscher straining at its chain foam at the corner of its mouth, rain bouncing on cobblestones and the silhouette of a man lit by a streetlamp, sheltering from the rain waiting.

The English-speaking monk made an announcement on the last night, I was surprised 'cos he seemed almost happy or something he said this dead famous aul monk had kicked the bucket and if we wanted we could all go to the funeral, it was on this island just off the coast where he lived most of the time there'd be buses going and everything. He said it was a privilege to be offered the chance to see the aul fella off and if we weren't doing nothing else we should seriously think about it. I didn't fancy going to a funeral what a downer after ten days of silence and yoga, I wouldn't of minded having a wee drink and a few laughs not going overboard or nothing just a wee reminder that although I liked the Buddhists I wasn't one myself.

It was either that or hang round the monastery for

a couple of days, they said we could if we wanted just to come down off the experience and chat amongst ourselves about what it was like, that sounded better to me but if the gorgeous redhead decided she wanted to go to the funeral then that's where I was going too. There hadn't been a word between us yet obviously but since we'd had our wee moment there'd been constant eye contact like we were both dying to get a hold of each other for an aul chinwag and maybe more besides. It was weird so it was flirting without saying nothing but good too, none of the usual aul nonsense. I just hoped it wouldn't be spoiled as soon as we opened our gobs sure I was dead worried she'd be Irish, that's all I need to fall for one of our own with some aul annoying accent from Galway or somewhere.

So the buses were waiting on the morning of the eleventh day for those who wanted to go to the funeral. It was weird hearing people's voices and all the accents from all over the world loads of people came up to say hello to me and to thank me for doing the funny reading from the aul Tripitaka, they said it made all the difference gave them a boost halfway through the ten days and helped them over the hump. I appreciated that and it was dead good having an aul yarn with people and hugging them and whatever, they felt like good friends like I knew them really well even though we'd never even talked to each other before.

The guy with the glasses who always wore black came up to me dead serious I'd thought he was German but he was a Yank turns out he was there with his fiancée, that must of been weird, I goes, but he says they stayed away from each other. His girl was friendly she wasn't that into the meditation and everything, she said she was only doing it for him. I asked him what the story was and he told me he'd been a medic in the army sent out with a bunch of other lads into the desert somewhere but he saw too much and he lost it eventually and had to get sent home. You'd never have thought to look at him he'd had a life like that, his girl was a soldier too he met her when he was in the hospital getting his head seen to she was there too just like him lost the plot the aul army's not for everyone like. They were getting married in Hawaii in a couple of months, it was good talking to them and I wished them the best of luck.

My neighbour in the next cell come over to see me too the aul fella he was dead educated, Norwegian he was, name of Knut. I'd never heard a name like that before, fucking brilliant I thought. I started laughing straightaway, aye pleased to make your acquaintance Knut, I goes, give us a hug big man I know you've been wanting one for a while, he gave a huge laugh himself and near broke my ribs he squeezed me so hard, you give me hope when I see you, he says, what do you mean, I goes, no one ever said something like that to me before, it stopped me dead in my tracks so it did. Whenever I look at you I see strength, he says, and I know that anything is possible, fuck me you wouldn't believe what happened I just burst into tears he grabbed me again and I put my head into his shoulder he smelled of pine of autumn, it's all right son, he says, I know how you're feeling we've all lost something or someone. I was sobbing like a wean into his neck it would of been dead embarrassing only there was a couple of other people greeting too.

It took me a few minutes to pull myself together, are you coming to the island, I says to him, he shakes his head, no I can't I'm afraid I have to go home to my family now they're waiting for me. I understand, I says, all the best to ye and sorry about wetting your shirt there, don't worry about it, he goes, you take care of yourself and take care of her too. I looked at him rubbing the tears from my cheeks with my balled-up fist, he raised one eyebrow at me, you know who I'm talking about, he goes. Aye, I says, I think so.

And there she was leaning on the side of the bus with her backpack at her feet and watching me. I went over and gave her the nod. She smiled and lifted her bag up as the driver come over to open the baggage compartment and she chucked it inside and says, I'll save you a seat.

Right, I goes, and said cheerio to Knut and the medic and his fiancée and took one last look at the monastery wondering if I'd ever come back. The redhead was waiting for me down the back of the bus, nice one, I was thinking, that's the seats I always go for too so I can get a good look at everyone. She patted the one next to her and I started laughing. What's so funny, she says.

Nothing, I goes, just thinking our first date's a funeral.

Not exactly dinner and a movie, she says, she had a

dead relaxed American twang not one of the aul nasal accents like I want a bay-gel and a cup of caw-fee, look I'm Lana, she says, sorry about all the staring for some reason I couldn't keep my eyes off you, God I shouldn't be telling you this should I wow it's weird talking isn't it? I'm not usually much of a chatterbox so I apologise in advance if I talk your ear off until we get there.

No problem at all, I says, I could listen to you talking all day, I'm Will by the way.

We're going to get along just fine aren't we, she goes.

Bet the house on it, I says, sure we might as well sign the marriage certificate right now what names do you think are good for boys?

She laughed then and her cheeks flushed but she didn't miss a beat, ooh, she goes, I always liked Carter what's your surname?

Fitzgerald, I says, having to think fast.

Fitzgerald, she goes, that's good I like that, Lana Fitzgerald yeah that works.

I don't know about Carter though, I says, Carter Fitzgerald he sounds like a film star from the forties.

Yeah, she goes, *Attack of the Killer Tomatoes* starring Carter Fitzgerald.

Ha ha, I says, killer tomatoes where'd you get that from.

It's an actual movie, she says, a spoof of those B-movies from the fifties.

It is not, I goes, you're having me on, serious, she says, I've seen it it's hilarious, away and fuck, I goes, then covered my mouth with my hand, sorry I says, I swear a lot too much really I'll try and keep it under control.

She bit her bottom lip then and gave me a look, no, she says, the way you say fuck is, well, whew is the aircon not working in here usually these buses have it turned up to the max. She waved her hand under her chin a big grin on her face.

Jesus, I goes, at this rate we'll never make it to the island.

Tell me about it, she says, I haven't come in ten days. It was her turn to put her hand over her mouth then, her eyes went wide, sorry did I say that out loud oh my God I can't believe I just said that, aye, I goes, anyway how about a change of subject, holy fuck I was thinking, there's going to be some fireworks tonight to celebrate yer man's passing.

If you asked me what else we talked about the rest of the trip I couldn't tell ye, the only thing I 'member noticing is that she didn't ask me about how it was growing up in Belfast or what I done there or why I was here it was more about what I liked and didn't like and what I thought of things she didn't seem interested at all in who I'd been, only how my mind worked. I suppose that was a hangover from the retreat bloody lucky really if she'd met me before we wouldn't of got on as well as we did. My head was clear now and we were able to yarn about the universe and how the world worked and the big questions. I quite liked that sort of talk, the hours flew by everyone on the bus was jabbering away glad to be talking again except a few people on their own trying to process the real world outside the monastery walls staring out the window watching the countryside go by.

The bus drove onto this aul rickety ferry once we got to the coast, it didn't look very safe but we made it over to the island all right, it was only a small one just a couple of wee towns not many people living on it but quite a few had turned out for yer man's funeral. We all piled out of the bus and grabbed something to eat at this wee stall in the market, they had Coke and everything normally I'm a Fanta man but me and Lana grabbed a couple of bottles fuck it was good stuff, I was buzzing after it just goes to show ye how being off the western food for a while makes a difference. Me and her dandered down with a couple of the others to see the funeral site. I thought it would just be an aul graveyard but yer man's dead body was lying out on this pyre in the open air for everyone to see.

What's this, I says, don't tell us they're going to set fire to him.

Lana shivered, I suppose so, she goes. I didn't think about it but of course they're not a Christian society they've got different customs and traditions surrounding death I guess, right enough, I says, this should be something to see then bit like a bonfire on the eleventh night, what's that, she goes, what's the eleventh night?

I shook my head, don't worry about it sure it's just a dumb thing the Protestants do back home, the night before the Orangemen do their marching they light big fires all over the place and burn an effigy of the Pope load of aul bollocks really just an excuse for a piss-up and a fight.

Yeah, she says, I've seen footage of them marching down Catholic streets on the news it's a bit weird I mean we believe in free speech and all but I can't see the Ku Klux Klan marching through Harlem you know?

I laughed at that, aye totally, I goes, it's a bit like that they're all head-the-balls back home, she liked that one, head-the-balls, she says, it means you're stupid from heading a soccer ball too much right?

How'd you know that, I goes.

I played as a midfielder all through high school, she says, soccer's really popular with girls in America, is that right, I says, sure I love knocking an aul ball around we should get one and have a game on the beach see who else wants to play.

What beach is this you're referring to, she goes, oh you know, I says, dead casual, wherever we go after this, maybe Ko Pha-Ngan sure that's not far from here.

Oh so we're off to an island together are we, she says, acting all coy.

Why, don't you want to, I goes, knowing full well she was just joshing me.

Sure, she says, once the barbecue's over here let's go.

I laughed at that, aye shame they don't sell marshmallows at their wee stall there sure they'd make a mint.

We knocked around with the others from the retreat for an hour or two waiting for the festivities to start and trying to keep our hands off of each other. Just as well there was no beach to go and lie on and no privacy to be had, there was a bit of a crowd formed for the send-off. Monks came in a procession and stood round and then started chanting, it was quite good, there must of been a few hundred people there to watch. Lana squeezed my hand when they put the torch to the pyre, the thing went up pretty quick it's not something you see every day or want to see really but the monks and the locals all loved it they were happy the complete opposite of what ye see at a funeral in the west with everyone greeting. They all believed he was away to a new life reincarnated as someone else starting over again, the fire was purging who he used to be sure I could identify with that at least.

When I looked round at Lana and she put her head into my shoulder her red hair was rising in the wind out behind her face and I could see the flames reflected in her eyes she was crying a wee bit but smiling too this was the start of something for the aul monk who'd died and for us too, we both felt it.

It was mad being on Haad Rin Nok beach a couple of days before the party kicked off sure that was the only way you could get yourself an aul shack if you left it too late there'd be ten thousand other fuckers trying to grab them. Ours wasn't too bad it'd seen better days like but sure it's only a place to throw your bag down and have a kip and a dump in private. There was a hammock on the balcony sure I never mastered them I was too big but Lana jumped right in no problem. She wasn't so keen on the bathroom squat-toilet situation of course, if you're not used to each other it's a bit embarrassing at first not exactly high romance considering the dodgy pad thais going around if you know what I mean. There was some sort of big fucking lizards crawling around in the roof too sure the first time I saw Lana half in the buff was when she come running out squealing an hour after we checked in. We were still circling each other nothing had happened even though it was pretty obvious something was going to we'd come here and rented a shack together after all and there was only one bed.

Anyway she went in to do her business I was hanging out on the bed trying to look nonchalant going through my stuff wondering if the DJs would play anything from the CDs I'd bought and next thing I hear this animal croaking noise. I knew it was geckos straightaway sure they're only small things it's not hard to work it out 'cos their call is just their name, geck-o geck-o geck-o that's what they say. I didn't mind it but if you never heard it before it's a bit of a what-the-fuck-was-that moment, it must of been loud in the bathroom too I suppose.

The door bursts open and Lana comes running out squealing her face all flushed, Will there's something in there, she goes, some creature.

You're all right, I says, it's just a gecko they're only wee lizards sure they won't do you any harm. It was a weird moment 'cos she was standing there with one fist clenched by her side and the other hand up at her mouth, biting on her thumbnail, she wasn't wearing nothing from the waist down I mean that's easiest when you're dealing with squat toilets but still it was a bit of a shock to see her ginger pubes for the first time under such circumstances, not exactly the way I'd been imagining.

Can you get rid of it, she goes. I just turned my palms up and shrugged, they're pretty fast and hard to catch, I says, and even if I did get him there'll be another one in there an hour later you'll get used to it they won't come near ye don't worry. I was staring at her fire crotch the whole time thinking fuck me I'm going to go wild with this one she must of seen me, what are you oh sorry, she goes, and puts one hand over her fanny, blushing.

Bit late now, I goes, the ginger cat's out of the bag, she pulled her hand away and starts laughing, yeah, she says, who cares anyway, and does a wiggle for me, you're going to be seeing it constantly the next few days and I mean constantly, is that right, I says, sure I don't think I can stand it much longer Lana why don't you slide on over her and introduce me to your wee friend.

Look it's not like me to be bashful or nothing but for some reason it feels out of order talking about those first few days when me and Lana were together. We pretty much stayed in the shack hiding under the mosquito net only getting dressed to go up into Haad Rin to buy bottled water and some scran. We were in the wrong place really, we should of went to one of those quiet wee islands instead of coming to party central but it didn't seem right at the time sure we hardly knew each other and after the meditation it was good being around people again and hearing their aul chatter even if it was all a load of bollocks and they were just a bunch of wankers mostly.

It might of been too intense if it was just the two of us out in some remote place, at least on Ko Pha-Ngan there was loads of people for us to mingle with if we wanted. The backpackers were arriving by the busload every day more and more of them for the aul full moon party a lot of dickheads really but some all right people too the aul Goa trance music crowd, Germans and Israelis with long hair and dusty feet. Me and Lana talked to these two German girls who said they were here for a *psytranceparty* it sounded like one big word the way they said it, that's the Germans for ye like very good at thinking up single words for big long awkward ideas. Every time you talked to one of them and said something like I sort of feel like dancing but I'm a bit tired at the moment maybe later sure you knew they had a word for that feeling. You are *müdetanzenmann*, they'd say, not exactly a language for whispering sweet nothings in someone's ear hole is it.

We started venturing outside a bit more then, the aul hippies were good craic and they took their music dead serious, some of them had been coming for years they were worried the whole thing was getting taken over by eejits and getting too commercial, it was hard not to argue like. Me and Lana would take a wee walk along the beach not as romantic as it sounds 'cos there was thousands of people about running wild and drinking Red Bull and vodka from buckets the stalls would sell. That's all it was just an aul plastic bucket the sort you'd build a sandcastle with as a kid, a handle so you didn't drop it and a dozen straws so you could suck the aul go-go juice down like nobody's business. No wonder everyone was wasted, at least when you finished your drink you could use the same bucket to throw up in very handy so it was sure the Thais think of everything.

We were like an aul courting couple arms round each other holding hands and all that, a bit soppy but sure I didn't care I was all for reinventing myself or maybe the Thailand was doing it for me sure I never expected that now. It was like we were on the outside looking in just the two of us in our own wee bubble if we weren't busy pleasuring each other we were out observing the madness as things built up to the big full moon party. Sometimes we'd just sit down at one of the wee food stalls and grab some noodles or something and watch the backpackers dancing about and getting pished it was quite funny so it was but also a bit sad, sure most of them were totally lost they didn't know who they were or what they were doing.

It's pretty hedonistic, Lana says to me, that's a good word, I says, are we living a hedonistic life then, sort of but in our own way, she goes, on our own terms it's weird but sometimes you step over a line in life like you wander off the path and all of a sudden you're in the forest and you see these other people walking along the path all going the same way with the same resigned expressions on their faces and you realise that was you a minute ago but now you can see it you can't go back even if you wanted to you can try stepping back onto the path and joining the rest except they're blind they can only see what's right in front of them but you, you can see the forest all around with the trees stretching up into the canopy and the tropical birds and all this cacophony you're part of that now and it's wonderful but how can you explain it to all these people on the stone path who can't see what you're seeing?

She was totally on the money right enough, how could I ever tell Big Jim and them ones about the world I'd seen there was no going back for me now sure it would be like being in prison I couldn't do it, what about if everyone you know is on the path, I says to Lana, does that not mean you're on your tod in the forest?

No one's ever alone in the forest, she says, running her fingers up the length of my forearm, there's always others you just have to find them but you'll know when you see them.

A wee shiver ran up my back even though it was still dead hot outside. Aye I know, I says, I know that now it's just I feel like the first of my kind or something like an aul explorer.

You'd be surprised, she goes, I've met a few like us but not many true enough that's why I had to leave Indianapolis.

That's right I keep meaning to ask ye what it's like there only your ginger bits keep distracting us.

Oh don't say that, she says, crossing her legs and blushing you'll light a spark in me again, I need a rest.

I don't really know where Indiana is, I goes, all I know is Indiana Jones, it must be a bummer if you live there and your name's Jones sure everyone would take the mickey asking ye where your temple of doom was and that.

What about the Indy 500, she says, you must have heard of that.

The car racing, I goes, aye right enough that's out your way isn't it, is that where your man Cruise done the *Days of Thunder*? That's a good aul movie so it is. What's his name, Cold Trickle or something?

Lana laughed, yes! she goes, Cole Trickle his character's based on a real driver, I was a pit girl one summer when I was seventeen that was bedlam you get treated like a whore but it was either that or the county fair and I couldn't stand another few months in the donut truck I can't even look at a donut now without retching. I don't mind a donut, I goes, in fact I wouldn't mind one right now I've an aul sweet tooth do you want to get some banana fritters or something?

I ordered dessert from the Thai lad he gave Lana a good looking-over couldn't help himself like but he near shite when I gave him a stare, two minute two minute, he says, aye hurry up you wee fucker, I goes, or I'll slap the lugs off of ye.

Lana goes, look they're mad not to mention totally drunk.

I looked round and there was a couple of Thai lads setting fire to a big skipping rope they were standing up on crates and they started whirling it round it looked good so it did only these pissed backpackers all ran in and started jumping over it or trying to anyway. They went round a few times before it would hit them in the gob and they'd scream and drop down to the sand. Everyone would laugh and cheer and then the rope would start up again round and round the flames leaving a trace in the air that was weird on the eyes. Fuck me, I says, that's a bit dangerous especially with all these combustible dreadlocks and what have ye in the mix someone's going to set their fisherman pants on fire and burn their arsehole.

Lana snorted and says, this explains the queue at the first-aid stall we saw earlier.

I was curious about the America I wouldn't mind going maybe so I says to her, did you just bail out of the Indiana as soon as ye could like? Doesn't sound like there was much going on there it's in the middle of nowhere is it not?

Ah, it's not too bad, she goes, after I left high school I got a job in a cocktail bar downtown, the money was good but it was long hours. It took me a while to save enough to hit the road.

Her parents were aul hippies she'd told me before, no money in the bank so no question of paying for her to go to college or nothing once she turned eighteen she was pretty much on her own but she didn't mind. You didn't see too many girls travelling by themselves but Lana had been on the go for a couple of years now, she was only a year younger than me sure she'd been mountain climbing in India and all sorts.

You must of put a fair aul bit aside to keep you going this long, I says, though don't be worrying about money now sure I've got more than I could ever spend.

Yeah, she says, you've been a bit mysterious about

that did you rob a bank or something not that it would bother me necessarily, she goes on, grinning.

Nah never no banks, I says, sure they're too hard just a couple of post offices and the odd bookies nothing major.

Did you ever shoot anyone, she goes, laughing. The way she said it threw me off guard and before I could stop myself it was out of me, course, I says, her eyebrows went up and I caught myself then, but you know most of them deserved it well maybe not most of them but some of them did anyway. Fuck sake, I was thinking, stop running your mouth or she'll be on the next fucking boat out of here.

Sure she just shrugged, I couldn't believe it. I shot a guy once, she goes, he followed me home from the bar and tried to jump me in an alley just around the corner from my parents' place.

I just stared at her struck dumb sort of thing.

He was a big bastard too, drunk and strong I wouldn't have stood a chance. Lucky I listened to Tyrone the bouncer rather than my dad.

Did he give you a piece to carry, I says, finding my voice even though it sounded dead quiet.

Glock 26, she nods. Compact and fits in your bag. Good if you've got small hands. She sniffs then and looks off into the distance down to the water's edge. Shot him twice, she says all confident like it was nothing, he didn't die though he had to have a liver transplant. He's still in jail, or at least he should be.

How old were you, I says.

Nineteen, she goes, it doesn't bother me or anything I mean I'm not one of these gun nuts or really messed up about almost being raped that's just what it's like in Indianapolis and either you stay there and carry a concealed weapon when you go out at night or you go live somewhere else. I left the year after and haven't really been back since. She changed tack then and a big grin broke out on her face, you know I collected My Little Ponies when I was a kid I had like a thousand of them, most of them still in their boxes.

Right, I goes, but what's that got to do with putting a cap in someone's ass? I put on my best American accent to try and lighten the mood but it wasn't very good like.

Oh that's how I can keep travelling, she says, they're worth a fortune to collectors especially if the boxes haven't even been opened. I left them with my cousin, he sells a bunch of them when I need money and puts it in my account.

I laughed dead loud, are you fucking joking, I says, you mean you're riding a wee pink horse round the world?

Yeah! she goes, ha ha I never thought of it like that, ride 'em cowboy!

I was in a right aul good mood after that wee talk, everything about this girl was falling into place for me sure she was ticking all the boxes she reminded me of Tanya only even better even more worldly or confident it takes a certain type of person to throw down on some big fucker who's trying to tear your clothes off in a dark alley, fucking Glock 26 she says, unbelievable like.

Here, I says to her, I know this aul full moon party stuff's a load of aul bollocks but since we're here sure we might as well get into it what do you think, totally, she says, let's cut loose and dance the night away a bit of hedonism never did anyone any harm after being cooped up in that retreat I'm just about game for anything.

We got ourselves a couple of drinks not the buckets sure that's for mugs but a couple of good cocktails with umbrellas in them and whatnot. We hunted down some of the trance people sure they stood out a mile only a few of the bars on the beach were playing that sort of music anyway a constant thrum it was, driving into your brain relentless like only in quite a good way it's hard to explain if ye've not experienced it. I wasn't totally sold but you have to admire anyone with specialist taste particularly when it comes to music. Anyway you could see some of the backpackers drifting towards that part of the beach curious like this wasn't a sound they were familiar with and when you're off your face it's sort of perfect it grabs ye by the shoulders and holds you up all night like a pal who never gets tired and wants to keep going sort of thing sure you feel like a puppet on a string.

Me and Lana were dancing a wee bit after a couple of drinks building up a sweat and trying to get into the music. I felt a wee bit out of place but it was all right sure there was plenty to look at flashing lights and fire twirlers and women in bikinis and fellas doing acrobatics or walking on stilts. Just when I was thinking fuck me I wish I had a couple of pills or a wee line of speed these three lads danced over towards us. They had good moves so they did obviously they were into it dead tan and skinny they were you could see their aul rippling sixpacks they had tribal tattoos on them too and big grins on their faces.

Right, I was thinking, these ones are on something I'd recognise that goofy expression and clenched jaw anywhere. I gave them the nod and leans in, bout ye lads, I goes, youse having a good night?

Fucking beezer mate, one of them says, putting his arm around my shoulder, course wouldn't you know it they were English.

I laughed to myself and took a deep breath, you like the trance then, I goes, unreal, he says, his eyes were rolling back in his head a bit, are you all right there, I goes, better drink some water or something you're sweating like a bastard. His eyes went wide then, oh thanks mate, he goes, I lost track there for a bit hey Richie, he says to one of his pals making a drinking motion with his hand, time out for a minute.

He put his arms right round me then sort of giving me a hug, you stay here mate all right we'll be right back we want to have a dance with you and your girlfriend you're nice people gorgeous couple you are, my name's Dave by the way sorry I'm a bit chatty and touchy-feely you know what I mean.

Aye no bother, I says biting my lip thinking, Dave Dave why'd he have to be called Dave he seems all right though try not to be prejudiced Will still getting used to calling myself that. Lana was throwing her hair all round and letting it hang down over her face it was brilliant in the moonlight and with all the fire reflecting off of it and that. She pushed it back out of her eyes and leans in to me still dancing, they looked like they were on X, she goes, I had to think about what she was saying for a minute, X aye right ecstasy good name for it, I says.

What do you call it, she goes, just pills, I says, or dancing batteries or Dambusters or red meanies, yeah all right all right, she goes, how many types have you got in Ireland? Loads, I says, we used to get them in bulk from Holland sure I always had a couple on me just in case. Just in case of what, she says, a house music emergency just in case Carl Cox pops round for lunch?

I laughed and goes, pretty much, we popped them like aspirin sure I'm dead used to them it takes a couple to get me going now, do you want me to ask these lads if they have any spare?

Well we're going to need something, she says, I'm not a drug fiend or anything but how often do you find yourself at a full moon party?

She had a point like. I waited till your man Dave come back with his mates Richie and whatever the other one was called, he was dead pleased to see me like we were aul pals or something. I told him our names and he give us both a big hug he was flying no doubt about it sure he'd probably not even 'member us in the morning. The third one was called Jez it turned out sure I could of guessed if they're not called Dave they're called Jez don't know what the score is there like, the mysteries of being English. They were all right actually quite good fun we started joshing each other good-natured like I asked Dave if he had any pills and he goes, sure no problem mate we brought loads over with us.

Are youse mad, I says, do you not know what the penalty is for that here in the Thailand life in prison, ah well, he goes, sure you only live once.

I had to laugh they weren't bothered at all, well just watch yourselves, I goes, if you see the peelers coming through the crowd just calm yourselves down and don't give nothing away these cunts will shake you down for everything you've got if they know you've pills on ye.

You're absolutely right, he goes, that's why we've got Jez on security detail, isn't that right Jezza.

Sure I looked at him and he was away with the fairies, aye good idea, I says, look sort us out and I'll watch your back I've a bit of experience if you know what I mean.

He thought that was dead funny for some reason and slipped us a couple of green pills, what are they like, I says, they're not bangers are they, no no, he goes, they're dead smooth a bit trippy but lovely just take half at a time though otherwise they'll come on too strong and you'll be spackered.

I gave Lana the wink and broke one in two for us after that it was just a waiting game she kept getting me to bend over so she could scratch her nails on my head and I kept rubbing her back, don't know if it makes any difference in it coming on but it feels good like.

The English lads thought we were great Lana starts chatting away to yer man Richie telling him all about how we met I didn't mind sure you either can't shut your gob or you shut it too tight when you're on a pill. Jez was on his own wee trip but me and your man Dave started an aul conversation sure I could feel the tendrils creeping up my spine the whole time it was dead good so it was.

Fucking awesome tatts, he goes, were you in prison in Northern Ireland like, even though I was starting to take off his question still surprised me the way he asked it all casual.

Nah, I says, I always managed to stay out of it but still they're a bit fucked I wish I didn't have them now having to explain that shite every time I take my shirt off sure yours are better, I goes.

Don't worry about it, he says, there's no one judging you for the past here we're all a big family, that's very nice of you Dave, I says, he said it so matter of fact I was a bit humbled he leaned in close then and whispered in my ear, I just want to say I'm sorry for what we did over there bloody typical empire-building sure everywhere we go we make a balls-up we should just stay out of other people's business.

I'd never heard the like of it honest to God. An Englishman apologising for his country, first time for everything sure he must of seen the look on my face 'cos he laughs and goes, come on mate we're not all cunts some of us go a bit deeper you know what I mean? Fuck it was a watershed moment for me I don't mind telling ye it was like the clouds parted and I could see clear for the first time that sounds corny as fuck but by the time yer man Dave was telling me all this something had a hold of my brain like a wee supernova exploding dead quiet in the back of my neck a warm shockwave marching up over my skull like thousands of wee My Little Ponies on the rampage, a herd of pink horsies descending into my eyeballs.

After that it was dance central sure Wacko Jacko had nothing on us the moves we were putting down right enough if anyone had stumbled onto Haad Rin Nok right then sure they'd think they were on the set of 'Thriller' or something, ten thousand people there must of been all dancing and throwing their arms in the air and whooping up an aul storm, it was magic so it was. I was dead happy dancing in the sand with my new friends and a gorgeous woman sure how lucky was I we were all hugging each other and telling each other how brilliant we were a load of aul bollocks I know but when the MDMA kicks in sure you don't wish a single person in the world any harm, that must be how the Buddhists feel all the time except without these mad rushes of serotonin in the brain whooshing over ye.

They were good aul pills so they were, nice and smooth like yer man said and all the lights and sweat and sand and the moon was a good combo for giving you a wee trip not much mind not like one of them Dali paintings or anything just a wee bit of altered reality sort of thing. I was getting a visual echo like seeing people moving in stages through the air their arms and heads still hanging in space even though they'd moved on, it was quite good but you had to be careful not to knock into people. Even if you did no one was bothered sure it was all sorry mate and give us a hug you big bastard ye.

Lana was bending the ear off of Richie he had an arm round her and I was feeling a bit funny about it but I know what it's like when you're off your face and talking to someone who's the same. Dave must of scoped me looking at them he hands me a bottle of water and says, don't sweat it mate Richie's the last one you need to worry about sure he's bent as a five-bob note.

I could hardly speak my jaw was grinding so much, what do you mean, I says, is he a bender, aye Dave laughs, course he is sure it's bleeding obvious could you not tell.

I looked over at your man Richie and shrugged, sure how could I tell, I goes, it's not like he's wearing leather chaps or something.

Yeah only on weekends, Dave goes, he's a right dirty bastard actually I walked in on him and this Thai lad two nights ago fucking hell mate what a shock that was not something you see every day know what I mean.

I laughed then, aye I can imagine, I says, burned on the aul retinas is it.

Jesus you've no idea, Dave goes, I mean I really opened the door at the wrong moment you know but what can you do he's a mate we went to school together.

Boarding school was it, I says winking, God no, he says, can you imagine Richie let loose in a boarding school sure no one would be able to sit down.

You on the prowl yourself, I goes, sure there's loads of gorgeous women around here, nah, he goes, I'm not bothered sure you end up spending half the night letching when you could be dancing and enjoying the music it's one or the other for me. When we're back home we always go to the gay clubs I mean it pleases Richie and me and Jez love the music and not having drunken tits in our faces all night. That sounds weird I know I probably sound like a woofter myself but the fact is mate I'd rather keep my sex life off the dance floor, know what I mean?

Aye well sort of kind of I was thinking, anyway I had this dead warm feeling in my stomach rising up into my chest it was quite powerful so it was and I pulled Lana away from Richie not aggressive or nothing just excuse me do you mind if I cut in sort of thing.

Will, she goes dead loud, squealing all happy like she'd forgot all about me and now here I was right in front of her, oh my God you should hear Richie's stories about what he does with the Thai boys, it's totally wild. She leans in to my ear, a bit gross she goes, but don't tell him I said that, it's not getting you worked up is it, I says smiling.

God I don't need Richie for that, she says, the combination of this X and you next to me is already a bit much I think I'd come if I kissed you at this stage.

Let's try out your theory, I says, and put the aul lips on her. Jesus it was like we were floating on a wee cloud the tingling sensation of her lips was electric and feeling her close to me with her arms wrapped around my back

I near burst into tears something was churning up in me all right my guts were doing backflips trying to get a perfect score from the judges.

Let's go back to the hut for a bit, she says, I want to rub myself all over you and maybe we could get some body paint and do a design on each other. I didn't even answer just grabbed her hand in mine and nodded at Dave, see you later lovers, he goes, as we pushed our way through the crowd. It was hard going it must of taken us fifteen minutes to get back to the aul shack stopping off to grab some body paint from one of the stalls the whole time it was like having two sponges tied to your feet just bouncing along like Buzz Aldrin and them ones on the moon.

We tore the clothes off of each other once we were inside sure it was dead dark there was no electricity or nothing in the huts but we left the front door open so the moonlight could come in a wee bit, the hut was up on stilts sure no one would bother us and God help them if they did. We were both dead sweaty and had the horn real bad but just being naked together and kissing and holding on to each other dead tight was enough, we tried having a bump but it's weird when you're on the pills your system doesn't work like normal you can't come or nothing or if you do it's hard won and almost hurts. We ended up just licking each other all over sure I was totally fascinated by her crotch she couldn't drag me away it must of been the same for her with my aul wang it was like she'd never seen one before and here was the most amazing thing in the world right in her hand.

Listen, I goes to her, there's things you don't know about me and I feel bad I feel like telling ye but it's not very nice so it's not I mean I grew up in a weird place and I didn't always do the right thing I hurt a few people you know and doing the meditation has brought it all up there's stuff inside me that's going to come out just warning ye if you're hanging around.

She put her fingers on my lips then and says, shush Will don't worry I'm not going anywhere and no matter what it is I won't be afraid. I know we haven't known each other for very long and it's probably just the X talking but I'm really feeling something for you and you know that's not like me at all I'm very cautious about who I open up to but there's something between us I can feel it I think we're going to be together for a while and if that's the case well I'm here for you.

Lana, I says, I'm with you all the way I feel the same I'm falling for you big time so I am and that's caught me unexpected so it has I'm just a bit worried it's pretty rough in there, I goes tapping my aul noggin, we'll worry about that later, she says, I think we've both been caught with our pants down on this one so to speak. Let's just enjoy tonight my love, and she kissed me dead deep and passionate, my head was spinning with pleasure so it was just the sound of her saying the word love shattered something inside my heart and there it was now like a fucking sunrise beaming out of my chest it was so hot and powerful I was sure if she let go of me and opened her eyes the whole room would be lit up, the whole beach, the whole world and everything would stop just for the glory of us.

We both of us done another half and then another one and then another two green trippers in total each. I'm not saying it was the best idea in the world like but sure when you're loved up you just want to keep going and for it never to end. The problem when you do a couple of strong ones like that is the night becomes a blur ten hours pass in what feels like about twenty minutes I mean I was out of it most of the time, walking around and dancing and snogging the face off of Lana and talking away to strangers and hugging them and telling them they were brilliant but if you asked me who I was chatting to about the space-time continuum or the early films of Scorsese or whatever sure I couldn't pick them out for a million buckeroos. I believe the English expression is munted, well and truly munted that was me all right brilliant night it was of that there's no doubt bit of a shame it was just a mash-up of wee memorable moments doesn't bear thinking about what them bangers do to your aul brainpan.

All I 'member is me and Lana dancing like mad ones under the moon like pagans or something I just had my shorts on and she was in her green bikini the both of us was covered in body paint too a right aul mess we were sure we thought it was brilliant at the time everyone else was the same, thousands of dodgy fluorescent smears all over people's tits and arses these things never look so great in the harsh light of day but you're so knackered by then sure you're past caring.

I think we saw the English lads Dave and Richie and Jez again I was talking to them for ages anyway so I hope it was them for all I know it might of been a couple of other boyos, doesn't matter I suppose. It got a bit crazy somewhere in the middle of the night there the music building to a crescendo sending people right off their heads everyone's arms up in the air all jumping up and down guldering at the top of our voices then the DJ brought it back down to chill everyone out then back up again Jesus sure this went on for hours up and down rushing and recovering, if them pills weren't designed for taking with electronic music sure who knows what they were for.

I don't know what time it was we hadn't a watch or nothing but it must of been late and there was an aul purple reddish light on the horizon the sun getting ready to take his shift sure the big moon had done his job sending us all doolally. Anyway a group of about twenty dancers ran into the water the waves were dead gentle they must of been sweating and needed an aul dip there was bikini bottoms and swimming trunks flying off in all directions once people saw loads of others joined in, fuck me it was some sight I'm just glad I 'member it.

Me and Lana stripped off and run in too there must of been a thousand naked people in the water all laughing and jumping about and grabbing each other some of them kissing and who knows what else. The shore was littered with abandoned trunks and bikinis of all colours like some container ship carrying beachwear had crashed on the rocks or something.

Everyone goes on about the sixties, I says to Lana, but it can't of been a patch on this. She was bobbing in the water next to me shivering a wee bit her nipples standing out a mile goose bumps all over her, yeah, she goes, probably something similar I guess only with hairier muffs.

I laughed, aye right enough hairy fanny's going out of fashion faster than tape Walkmans next thing we'll all be looking like robots. She smiled and I could see she was a bit tired the aul bangers were wearing off I was on a plateau so I was feeling nice enough but not much happening now.

God I'm cold all of a sudden, Lana goes.

Move around a bit in the water, I says, that'll warm ye up sure we'll get out in a minute.

Good luck finding your shorts, she goes, and leans back in the water to lie on her back.

I looked back at the pile of clothes on the shoreline

about nine thousand people tramping over them and thought, fuck it I'll just walk back to the hut in the buff sure I don't care.

I turned round and Lana was floating in the wee gentle waves her body this long white shape like a swordfish or something except her red hair was all splayed out in the water loads of it there was, tendrils with a life of their own like some big jellyfish attached to her head or a bloodstain. As soon as I thought that I got a wee flash before my eyes of our Mark lying on the ground, dead disturbing so it was I shook my head to make it go away but there was something funny going on inside me. Fuck, I thought, these aul pills are giving me hallucinations or something. A wave came in then and Lana rose right up her body riding it she was like a corpse there in the water all pale and cold the wave hit me side on and splashed me in the face.

I staggered a bit and spat out water another image appeared in front of me then, rain hitting my cheek me standing over someone freezing and furious. I slapped myself in the gob and whispered, fuck sake Billy what's wrong with ye pull yourself together it's just the start of an aul comedown you've had them before don't lose the plot big man.

Lana, I says, making a grab for her leg, come on let's go back, she stood up in the water then her brow furrowed as she looked at me.

Are you all right Will, she says, aye, I goes, I'm just having a wee bad moment here, something hit me then like a spasm in my spine, fuck, I shouts and swallows real hard giving Lana a look.

Let's go now, she says and puts her arm under mine. We waded back into shore there was people all around whooping and cheering at all the nudies coming in and out of the water and looking for their kit, we just ignored them and even though the two of us were buck naked we splashed our way along the waterline back towards the huts. People were staring at us but they must of seen the look on my face like I was sick or something a few good sorts helped us along and told others to get the fuck out of the way I'll say that for your dance music crowds they help each other out if someone's not right or having a wee episode.

The sun was rising over the horizon people were starting to sit down and appreciate it I could feel the first warm feeling of it on my skin I'm sure it was beautiful and all but I'll tell you what even though it was just an aul wooden shack with a sweaty mattress and a torn mosquito net I've never been so glad to get home. Lana was practically carrying me towards the end my legs were going all funny dead stiff I was seizing up or something.

Shouldn't of made that crack about robots, I says weakly, trying to make a joke.

Just shut up, Lana goes, lie down I'll take care of you it'll be all right I'm here.

I'm sorry, I says, seriously whatever I say I'm sorry you've got to believe me please don't leave please.

Fuck me, I never thought it would come down to just one day when I'd have to face up to what I done but that's the way it turned out. No magistrate or court of law or nothing, must of been my own conscience or our Mark reaching out from beyond the grave or wherever the fuck he was. I was caught with my guard down after having all the pills sure you're always a wee bit vulnerable after a big night. I was totally defenceless when it happened not prepared or nothing but it's my own fault I suppose I should of worked it out ages ago but you know how it is always putting things off especially if you know deep down they're gonna be a fucking nightmare.

That's how it started actually, an aul nightmare. Me and Lana were exhausted the two of us I was getting wee flashbacks and not feeling the best and she was fussing over me, she soaked her towel in cold water and folded it up for my head to try and keep me cool I was drifting in and out of consciousness sort of a half-sleep half-drug fever comedown sort of thing. Eventually she must of passed out too poor darlin' she must of been knackered. I started having these aul vivid dreams my eyes was opening and closing sure I don't know what state I was in then it all started flooding back there was no way of me resisting no more.

There I was in the back of a van with Big Jim and our Mark and another fella, Talbot his name was though we called him Tabby. It was all dark and wet in there and we were arguing Big Jim was telling me we had no choice my brother was a squealer he'd been talking to the wrong people and telling them all about our operations that was why he was tied up on the floor with an aul gag in his mouth his eyes wide glaring at me as if to say don't believe it Billy sure you know I wouldn't do that. I was defending him and telling Big Jim no way not our Mark it can't be it must be someone else this is a mistake. Big Jim looked huge in the dream, he'd a black jacket on him and a Browning 9 mil. in his belt, are you defending this cunt, he says, you better watch it Billy or I'll be turning my gaze on you this makes me question your loyalties.

Tabby kicked our Mark in the guts then and I slapped him one with the back of my hand my ring burst his lip, don't you fucking touch him, I says, that's my brother if he's done anything wrong I'll deal with it not you.

Mark's gag came out then and he shouts, no Billy please I didn't know and Big Jim gives me a look as if to say I fucking told ye so then clubs him with the butt of the pistol, that's when I woke up completely dripping with sweat.

I sat up straight on the aul bed and turned around so my legs were hanging off the side of it trying to touch the wooden floor. Lana was lying there spread-eagled all sweaty her eyes closed out for the count, fuck me I was thinking, that was horrible so it was.

I kept seeing what happened next in my head I tried shutting my eyes but it wouldn't go away for a minute I thought maybe I was still sleeping but I wasn't this was real like I was reliving it I knew what was coming, oh fuck, I says out loud, it was like being tied to the tracks of a rollercoaster just waiting for it to come squealing round the corner and chop ye to bits.

We were in the shooting yard. That's where we'd take Catholics if we wanted to do a number on them and where we'd get young ones initiated into the cause by handing them all a piece with one bullet in it and getting them to shoot someone who was strung up to the wall. Get five lads to do it at once and the responsibility's shared and if someone doesn't pull the trigger then you break his fingers. I'd been there myself years before, it was a bad place so it was a lot of poor cunts had come to a nasty end on those cobblestones and here was our Mark lying on the ground bleeding from the mouth and the ears after a beating. It was raining and

Big Jim was arguing with Tabby under the awning whilst I stood over Mark with blood on my knuckles. Big Jim had convinced me Mark was a squealer, he had proof right enough and I'd got stuck into him. I knew where this had to go but my brain couldn't process it all I could see was my wee brother lying in the rain with his head kicked in and 'membered him pushing me down Tennant Street on the go-kart we made out of aul pram wheels we'd pinched. I couldn't hardly believe he'd squealed on us but Big Jim laid it all out there was no denying it and I was raging so I was.

Tabby was pleading for my brother's life which is what I should of been doing instead of standing there like a dumb cunt but whatever he was saying to Big Jim wasn't filtering through and next thing my boss steps out from the shadows the rain dripping off his chin and extends his hand to me. It was the Browning. I took it and fuck me I don't know if I can even say what I done Jesus fucking Christ I said goodbye to my wee brother Mark like he was nothing to me even though he was everything he was all I had left and I fucking shot him, oh God help me I shot him what did I do that for why didn't I stop and say no oh Jesus mother of God why.

I stood up in the hut pulling at the mosquito net to get it off of me and my whole body went stiff as a board fucking rigid like I'd been electrocuted. I tried to shout scream make any noise at all but there was nothing came out of me, I could hardly breathe my lungs were so tight in my chest, I could feel the muscles in my neck straining and my eyes bulging and then it was like something shot out of me through the fucking roof and I collapsed on the floor like an aul sack of potatoes no feeling in me at all.

I lay there for a couple of minutes catching my breath not even able to think about what was happening I was so feared and then slowly at first I started crying it all came pouring out of me built up for years and I couldn't stop I just couldn't and I didn't want to neither.

Lana must of heard me because next thing you know there she was on the floor beside me the two of us naked as jaybirds all sweat and stink sand and dirt sticking to us still salty from the sea, she held on to me real tight whispering in my ear her voice dead soft and comforting. She didn't even know what was going through my head but she knew it was bad sure there was no mistaking it honest to God how she put up with me those next few hours I'll never know there's a lifetime of debt right there. She tried to get me up on the bed but I was dead weight so I was, so she pulled the sheet and pillows down onto the ground to try and make me comfortable stroking my head the whole time she was and singing wee lullabies like you would for a wean who's having a rough night.

I lay on the floor bawling my eyes out for hours, it was as low as I've ever felt in my life it was like all the shite I'd ever done got converted to tears there must of been about three gallons of salty water came out of me even though it was warm I was shivering and curled up in a ball under the sheet Lana scooched in behind me. Every time I thought I was calming down it started up again only worse. I just wanted to die that's the truth of the matter, that's all I deserved I was thinking.

The shooting yard was gone out of my head now or at least something was different about it I just 'membered Mark growing up and how he was and all the things between us as dumb fucking wee lads how he used to go mad if I threw the cardboard cylinders inside bog rolls in the bin when he liked to collect them to build castles and how he licked the lids of yoghurts which disgusted me a wee bit sure he'd do it right in front of me and that time when he come home with a pair of red slip-on shoes with tassels on them and I near died laughing. Him dyeing his hair jet black but not realising you had to keep the dye from getting on your skin and ending up with a black forehead and streaks all down his back. The time our da got him an aul second-hand racing bike with ten gears it was a bit big for him but Mark went out on it anyway pleased as punch and some fucking stupid cow couped him off it with her Datsun a week later when she come out of a side street without looking the bike was wrecked and he had a broken wrist, fucking lucky he was her too it goes without saying. Him buying his first album, Frankie Goes to Hollywood *Welcome to the Pleasuredome* he played it about a thousand times, sure 'Two Tribes' was our anthem I still 'member all the tracks and most of the words Holly Johnson singing *In Xanadu did Kubla Khan a stately pleasuredome e-rect*.

Every wee moment of him that came back started me bawling afresh I didn't get no sleep at all that day, sure

I never thought I'd sleep again but by about three in the afternoon I was wrung out there was no more tears left in me, that's not to say I was done being upset sure I knew the feeling would never go away when I thought about our Mark but for the first time it felt like I actually could think about him and 'member the good bits of how he was, the knowledge was there of what I'd done there's no denying it but at least I wasn't trying to deny it no more it was something I'd have to live with even though it's the worst thing in the world and you can't imagine going on living the fact is you are living waking up and eating and walking around and talking to people and experiencing the world and going to your bed the cycle never ends and you can't help that it's the way it is and you can stay sorry about something your whole life God knows I knew I'd think about my brother every day from now on and have a wee quiet moment remembering him and telling myself what a cunt I was back then but I never wanted to hurt no one no more and I realised I wasn't that cunt anymore the man I was now was different, sure every day you're different as you move further away from who you used to be people say you have to learn from the past and the mistakes you made but I don't agree with that so I don't, it's not by reliving the past that you'll learn anything it's by living in the present like the Buddhists say fuck me they're totally right about all this stuff so they are.

My face was all puffed up and my legs felt like two melting ice-creams but by the time evening was coming around Lana managed to get me up and into the bed I was totally wrung out she was too but it felt like I might be able to sleep a wee bit out of pure exhaustion. She flopped back on the bed rubbing her eyes and I squeezed in beside her our skins sticking to each other, thank you I says about to pass out she just nodded and smiled she was a bit teary herself tell me about him one day, she goes, her voice all croaky. I must of been muttering away all day about our Mark I gulped it near set me going again with the waterworks, I will, I says, I will my love.

The two of us fell asleep holding onto each other then, the last thing that went through my mind was I'm never letting this one go that's the end of the old me right there when I close my eyes when I wake up my new life begins. We must of slept for six hours or more sure when I opened my eyes again it was the middle of the night and all was quiet there was no aul party going on I suppose everyone was knackered and crashed out like us. I got up dead wobbly and stared at Lana for a bit in the gloom just her outline perfect she was absolutely perfect sure she'd stuck with me through this seen me at my worst and I knew I could trust her, maybe the first I ever could. I'd never do better and I vowed to 'member that. I was dead hot and needed some air so I went outside onto the wee balcony looking down over the beach and the ocean. There was no one about only a few last gaspers further down the beach the music was all switched off and there was rubbish everywhere bottles and food wrappers and bits of clothing, what a mess. The sky was clear it was quite bright 'cos the aul moon was out again and nearly full sure just on the wane now you could almost see the craters on it the sea of tranquillity and all that there was loads of stars too, nothing like looking at infinity for calming ye down.

I stood there on the balcony staring up at space thinking none of this meant nothing anyway worrying about our Mark and the past and whether I was a bad man or not sure I'd be gone soon too maybe next week or next year or in fifty years and a while after that this beach would be gone washed away probably no sign of the parties that went on the debauchery the madness. Everyone who ever came here would be gone too and nobody who was still living would 'member none of it.

The jungle behind us was alive with sounds I could hear a hundred thousand insects rubbing their wings together all oblivious to my aul problems sure I was nothing just nothing I didn't matter and sure that was all right so it was that's the way it is, goodbye Mark, I says out loud, goodbye brother maybe one day I'll see ye again maybe one day we'll be together save a spot for me if you can see your way to forgiving me I've changed now I promise I promise you Mark I've changed. Believe me you have to believe me I'm sorry brother.

An aul itching sensation on my ankle woke me up and I reached down to scratch at it letting my eyes open dead slow like. For a couple of seconds sure I'd no idea where I was and raised my head from the pillow to get a better look at the woman I was lying next to. Then I 'membered.

Lana had kicked off the sheet and was lying on her front with her head facing away from me, her long hair was splayed all wild across her back so's I couldn't even see her shoulders. I propped myself up on one elbow I was all groggy so I was blinking the sleep away my brain going mental in wonder at the woman I had before me. I ran my eyes down over her back to her arse, she had one leg pushed up at an angle like she was trying to climb a rock face or something amongst the sheets.

Even though I'd just woke up from a really deep sweaty

sleep after about four hours of bumping the night before I started to get hard again when I looked between her legs at the wee tangle of ginger hair just visible above her dead smooth fanny lips. Very distracting so it was, I looked away down her legs and examined the burn mark on her shin from where she pressed it against the exhaust of the aul moped we'd hired a couple of days ago. Bloody sore but sure everyone does it half the people we'd met on Ko Tao had them it's like a mark of respect or something you've earned your stripes sort of thing.

I felt bad at the time 'cos we'd only gone into town to buy some postcards Lana couldn't be bothered but I wanted to send one to Tanya out in Australia just to thank her for opening my eyes to a different world, is she an old flame, Lana says eyebrows arching, aye something like that, I goes, you're not jealous are ye, not one bit, she snorts, you're all mine now.

There was no arguing with that, we had a wee drink and I persuaded her to send a card to her parents just to tell them she was all right and that, she gave in and fired one off I wrote a few words on it myself BOUT YE'S! in big letters. They'll be delighted to see I've finally found a man, Lana goes dead sarcastic, sure leave them alone, I says, we'll pop in and see them in a few months if you're not sick of me by then, oh they'll love you, she goes, aye who wouldn't, I says, sure I'm gorgeous so I am.

There was loads of other couples busying themselves around the wee resort planning excursions and being shown how to use water-sports equipment by local lads looking dead worried they were going to wind up with a disaster on their hands. Lana scribbled down the details of how to get to this isolated waterfall out in the forest from the barman, it made me laugh watching him stand close to her I could see him inhaling that little bit harder than normal to capture her scent and I couldn't blame the young fella for sure you wouldn't get many exotic birds like this landing on your island very often.

Lana went back to the hut to get a wee backpack ready making sure we'd have enough water for the trek, even though yer man assured us we could refill our bottles at the falls I didn't want to take any chances the chalet we were staying in was nice and everything but it was still small enough to embarrass either of us if we wound up with an aul stomach bug sure it was a bit too early in the relationship to be confronted with the skitters and the mood was too good to be spoiled by having your arse hanging over the squat toilet all day.

The barman was hovering around giving me the eye and looking at me dead funny. I gave him the nod and says, what's the craic pal, this aul waterfall worth the trip or what?

Ah I thought so, he says grinning, you are from the north of Ireland, no?

I didn't see that one coming.

How'd you know that, I goes, feeling a wee twinge in my guts.

There was a guy here a few days ago who spoke like you. He had tattoos like yours.

I took an aul deep breath and lifted my T-shirt so he could get a good look. Like these, I says, are ye sure?

Yes, almost the same. He had this NO SURRENDER also, only it was around his arm.

The blood must of drained from my face because yer man looks all concerned and says, are you okay friend?

Aye, I'm all right, I goes, my mind racing to think who on Big Jim's crew had a tatt like that. Sure it could of been any one of the younger lads. I tried to play it cool.

What was he doing out here, do you know? Just on the holidays, was he?

The barman shrugged, sorry I don't know.

I thanked the lad and walked back to the hut to fetch Lana, my heart thumping. I knew it was probably nothing, just a weird coincidence, but all the same it made me think I'd have to seriously consider fucking off out of the Thailand for good. I didn't want nobody coming after me or trying to drag me back home sure that was the last place I wanted to go.

Lana's map said we had to hike along the beach and climb around the rocks until we found a track leading up into the hills. I made sure she was smothered in a thick layer of sunscreen before setting out even though she whinged about it sure I didn't want her all burnt. It took us about an hour's walking to round the point, a boring aul scramble over sharp rocks that was only livened up a bit by the sight of a sea snake lurking in the shadows. I wanted to get a close-up photo but Lana dragged me away in case I got bit, probably smart sure you wouldn't last ten minutes they're dead venomous so they are.

The heat of the afternoon wasn't too bad under the forest canopy but it was still dead humid, loads of people must of taken the trail before 'cos the walking track through the undergrowth was dead clear sure we'd only been hiking for about another half hour when we came across another exotic creature. I couldn't believe it I was dead excited even more than with the snake, it was a big black scorpion blocking our path. Lana was scared shitless but I poked it with the walking stick I'd made from an aul fallen tree branch. Lana near had a fit she shrieked and pulled me back as the scorpion raised its pincers in a display of aggression it was about the size of your fist so it was.

I just want to see him striking get off me will ye, I goes, it's awesome isn't it, don't annoy it Will, she goes, I don't want to have to carry you all the way back if it bites you.

They don't bite, I says, and besides it's probably dead venomous too so you wouldn't have to carry me far. I edged my stick towards it and the wee fucker wheeled around to try and see what was going on.

Will don't! Stop it, you're scaring me, Lana says, what if it takes a run at you? I hesitated for a second then pulled my stick back, I never thought of that can they run fast, I goes, how many legs has it got, she says.

I tried counting them, eight by the looks of it, I goes, right, she says, well that's four more than both of us put together come on let's go back this is obviously his forest, take it easy will you, I says, this is not Super Mario Brothers he's not some guardian we have to defeat to get to the next level. I'll just give him a wee incentive to move along out of our way with my trusty poking stick here. The scorpion scuttled away to the left to avoid the end of my stick then seemed to lose interest in us as it noticed something else in the jungle it turned sudden like and made its way quickly off into the brush.

The forest was quite dense sure you could hardly see very far into it all branches hanging down and moisture in the air very authentic so it was like in *Jurassic Park* or something. Straightaway I thought of yer man the great white hunter getting caught out by the raptors that was the best bit when he knows he's gonna get ate but admires them enough to say clever girl.

The two of us was stood there taking in the sounds of the jungle like fucking Tarzan and Jane, the sweat dripping down my back and soaking my T-shirt. I felt Lana's sweaty palm slip into mine and our fingers closed together dead tight. She was staring up at me with this weird expression, sort of studying me or something. I turned with my back to the forest so's I could see her in the sun and just bask in her aul beauty. We stood like that for a while just looking at each other no talk or movement or nothing just holding hands the two of us.

Eventually she moved in close to give me a hug, she stood up on her tippy-toes and her head went over my shoulder I was ready to squeeze the life out of her only she stepped back again dead quick and I was a bit disappointed until I saw the look on her face. She let go of me and put both hands up to her mouth. I could tell straightaway from her expression something was very wrong I'd seen it too many times back in Belfast that look of pure fear.

There was something behind me I could feel it there in the jungle I hadn't heard it sneak up I suppose that's its business not being heard, wouldn't be much of a predator otherwise. Lana was frozen to the spot so I turned around dead slow and peered into the gloom, it took me a few seconds to see it I think it was disbelief more than anything else that made me not register it was there sure it was pretty obvious.

A fucking tiger. It was huge, bigger than me and loads heavier just standing there poised like a house cat stalking a mouse or a bit of string waiting for it to move so it could open its mouth and leap. It was stunning so it was the first thing that went through my mind was holy fuck would you just look at that, fucking magnificent it never even occurred to me that I was about to get ate like yer man in *Jurassic Park* funny I'd just been thinking about that fuck sake what a stupid thing to be thinking when you're faced with two hundred kilos of killing machine, course I thought all this in about a millisecond or something 'cos after that my first instinct was to get between the animal and Lana.

Something kicked in then some switch inside me I went into pure concentration mode not scared or nothing dead calm actually they say you shouldn't look an animal in the eye like a gorilla in case it charges ye but that all went out the window, maybe it's not the same for big cats but I just took one small step to the side to block it from getting to Lana, flexed the muscles in my neck and stared it straight in the eyes.

Everything came into sharp focus then, it was just me and the tiger looking at each other studying each other sort of communicating and the only thing I could hear was the sound of my breathing and its breathing, its belly rising and falling its shoulder blades sticking up ready to pounce there's no way I could of stopped it if it had decided to barrel through me but I was talking away to it through my eyes I don't know how I done it but that's what it felt like, I want her, it was saying to me, no I said back, go about your business elsewhere you can tell what I am, you know I am not afraid brother. Wild so it was, never felt nothing like it, the creature kept staring at me with its big golden eyes its whiskers twitching a wee drop of moisture hanging off the edge of one clear as day it obviously heard what I was saying, I seen its shoulders relaxing ever so slightly. It's not that it couldn't take me of course it could easy but there was something between us some sort of understanding or respect maybe one beast acknowledging another, anyway it opened its mouth and bared its teeth turning its head sideways and snarling I tell you what ninety-nine point nine nine per cent of cunts in this world would of shit their pants right then and it would of been all over but I just smiled, nothing could hurt me no more I was gone beyond the limits somewhere more than human in that one perfect moment fucking transcendent so it was somehow everything was clear and in focus and still. I nodded and the tiger turned around and with a swish of his tail loped off into the jungle.

I waited for about ten seconds to make sure he was gone even though I knew he was. I turned round to Lana her eyes was wide her mouth hanging open arms limp by her sides. I put my hand on her hip to steady her, she was in shock obviously she looked up at me and swallowed her breath all shallow, she blinked once or twice trying to comprehend what she'd just seen. I couldn't blame her like it hadn't sunk in with me either. She lifted her clammy palm to my face and cupped my aul stubbly jaw with it.

I'll never leave you, she goes.

I know, I says. I caught her as she went down scooped her up in my arms red hair cascading over my chest like fire. She might not know everything about me but she knew enough, more than anyone and I knew she'd stay with me no matter what we were together now come what may.

A bunch of trackers came through five minutes later, they were beating the undergrowth with big sticks and a couple of them had dart guns, they went mad when they seen us, shouting and carrying on.

Aye take it easy, I says, how were we supposed to know there was a fucking tiger on the loose sure there's no signs or nothing.

Lana was recovered a bit by then we were sitting down having a drink of water and trying to decide if we should turn back or not. No mention of getting devoured in *Southeast Asia on a Shoestring*, she goes.

I laughed even though it wasn't funny really, where the fuck'd the tiger come from, I says to one of the trackers who was trying to tell us to go away in broken English, escape, he says, private zoo for tourists, youse are fucking mad in this country, I goes, your tiger went that way if you're looking for him.

That set them all going again shouting and guldering at each other and off they went after the beast.

I feel like sending them the wrong way, Lana goes, giving it a chance to get away.

Aye I thought of that too, I says, only what if it claws the face off of someone or snaffles up a wean better they catch it.

I hope they don't hurt it, she says.

I felt the same even though we'd just faced it down and could of been its breakfast.

Should we go on, I says. Lana stood up then, definitely, she goes, I don't believe in going back.

A wee trickle of water crossed the track about a mile further along and we followed it upstream as per the barman's instructions stepping from stone to stone at first but eventually not worrying about getting our shoes wet and just splashing through the shallows, the water was dead clear, we made better time that way and by about three o'clock we could hear the waterfall up ahead. The canopy opened up above us then allowing the sun to come through and as we moved out of the shade I stopped and dropped the pack so's I could peel off my aul T-shirt, it was soaking so it was. I stood in the sun for a bit arms spread wide to soak up the heat. Lana came and stood beside me on a flat rock wobbling slightly as she did the same she had a new bikini on underneath her T-shirt she held her hands out straight and wafted air under her arms, there was big sweat patches on her T-shirt and red strap marks on her shoulders where her pack had been.

I stuffed my soaking-wet T-shirt into the bag and fished out a bottle of water that was almost empty, I drank half of what was left and offered the last of it to Lana her hair had gone dark where it was stuck to her forehead and ears she looked like she needed a wee bit of refreshment sort of thing.

The waterfall was a bit disappointing after such a long aul hike through the jungle but we were still glad to have found it the water was flowing dead slow over a two-metre-wide shelf in the rock face then plunged about another ten metres into a shallow pool below, from there it dandered through a series of rocks down to the stream we'd been following to get there, not exactly Niagara Falls, Lana goes.

Have you been there, I says, I always fancied it.

Yeah, she goes, once when my parents took us on a trip to Canada an old friend of my dad's was working in Toronto. I was about twelve. You can get really close to the drop it's pretty amazing though a girl had jumped the day before we got there.

You're kidding me on, I says, does that happen often like?

I guess so, she says, I mean if you're going to kill yourself it's a pretty dramatic place to do it.

Youse Americans love the drama don't ye's.

About as much as we love the Irish, she goes, so out

of the blue I grabbed her around the waist and lifted her up and waded into the water she let out a big shriek and batted her fists against my chest but she couldn't stop me from dunking her in the pool. I was laughing as she stood up waving her arms and shaking the water from her hair, right you're dead, she goes.

She took a lunge at me and I stepped back to try and get out of her way but I slipped on the aul mossy bottom of the pool and sat down on my arse in the water. Lana cackled as she splashed me but I stood up dead quick and scampered back to the rocks, fuck sake, I says, you could of waited until I had my trunks on.

It's funny how you call them trunks, she goes, you're not that well endowed you know, is that right, I says, and I suppose you're an expert in these matters are ye?

I am a young woman of some experience yes, she goes, aye right, I says, I don't want to know about that thank you very much.

My shorts were soaking so I undid the buttons and took them off underwear too which got me a wolf whistle from Lana who was floating on her back and watching me. I laid them out on a rock in the sun and turned to strike an aul corny body-builder pose. Not bad, she says, God you're tan it's so annoying.

I waded back into the pool and leaned forward to start swimming sticking my tongue out as I passed her heading for the falls. She went back to shore and took off her own shorts and bikini draping them dead careful next to my clothes on the rocks. She stood in a star shape next to the pool then throwing her head back to the sky, at last we can get naked here, she says, there were too many people around at the resort.

I'd reached the falling water and pulled myself up onto a rock, streams of cold liquid poured down over my head and shoulders shocking me into taking sharp breaths. I tensed up against the sudden drop in temperature and watched Lana through the spray of the waterfall, a pink X against a backdrop of green and blue a wee triangle of orange at her centre. The aul camera shutter closed in my head, that was when I knew for certain what I was going to do and what direction my life was about to take and I defy anyone not to make the same choice.

Big Jim and others like him would always be out there, part of my past maybe but never far away. Yer man with the Loyalist tattoos turning up at the bar was like some aul spectre hanging over me. I had to get as far away as I could if I was ever going to put that world behind me.

It was simple in the end really. I just wanted to go on, make something of my life, go somewhere new and make a home, to love and protect this woman till her dying day, to raise a son maybe call him Mark and let him be the best man he could be.

I want to live, and I'll never surrender.

The author would like to thank:

David Winter: Editor, supporter, moustache model.
Jane Novak: Publicist, supporter, sophistication model.
Michael Williams: Honest early draft reader, beard model.
Josephine Rowe: Friend, Josephine Rowe model.
James Bradley, Nick Earls, Adam Levin, Wells Tower, DBC Pierre: Writers, supporters, terrible role models.
Jemima: Kittytorial suggestions, cute fluffy model.
Eirian Chapman: Centre of Universe, catwalk model (pending).

NO SURRENDER

ATIGERINEDEN.COM